BREATHING BOOKS

D0685643

This book is a work of fiction. Names, characters, places, and incidents are the product of the author's imagination or are used fictitiously. Any resemblance to actual events, locales, or persons, living or dead, is coincidental.

Copyright © 2018 by Cornelia Funke
English translation copyright © 2018 by Cornelia Funke

All rights reserved. In accordance with the U.S. Copyright Act of 1976, the scanning, uploading, and electronic sharing of any part of this book without the permission of the publisher is unlawful piracy and theft of the author's intellectual property. If you would like to use material from the book (other than for review purposes), prior written permission must be obtained by contacting the publisher at permission@breathing-books.com. Thank you for your support of the author's rights.

Second Edition: June 2018

10 9 8 7 6 5 4 3 2 1

Book design by Mirada
Printed in Canada

THE WILD CHICKS
class trip
CORNELIA FUNKE

PREFACE

I am often asked whether I base my stories on my own life. "Well," I mostly answer, "I usually don't ride dragons or step through magical mirrors. But there is this series, which caused thousands of German girls to walk around with feathers around their necks, build tree houses and chicken coops and…look for boys they could call the Pygmies. One of its characters is based on the mean grandmother of my mother, and I used everything I know about growing up in 1980s Germany for these books: about loving parents, bad parents, jealousy and friendship and…chickens of course!"

I love to write fantasy, so why did I ever write girls' books (which I never read when I was young)? Because one day my editor said: "Cornelia, would you write a book without dragons or fairies for a change?"

"Why?" I responded. "That would be terribly boring."

"Please try. Just one," she said.

So I sat down, and the Wild Chicks were born. Soon I got letters like: "Please Cornelia! Make the world a better place! Write another Wild Chicks book!" or "When I get sad, I just have to touch the Wild Chicks book I keep under my pillow." Those letters were so irresistible that I wrote another and another and another…eventually, they were turned into movies in Germany and, when I do events, young German women come up to me and whisper: "I was a Wild Chick. Thank you!"

I wonder what American girls will think of these books — there are no mobile phones, and the heroines are done with school by 2pm at the latest. They are all Northern German by descent, which was the reality of the small suburban towns I grew up in during the eighties, but luckily I've learned that most readers find something of themselves in one — or all! — of the girls, no matter their background, race, or sexuality, which is once again proof that we are all not that different. If my stories remind some readers of that truth, my job as a writer is done.

So…please let me know how you like my girls. And the boys of course. A boy once said in a reading. "Thank you, Cornelia! One can learn everything about girls reading *The Wild Chicks*." I admit that was never my intention, but books do have a way of telling the stories they want to tell.

With love to all the wild girls in the world,

P.S. This is the second adventure and there are more to come!

CHAPTER 1

"In here!" Charlie shouted, pulling open the compartment door. "Quick! Hurry!" She threw her bag on one of the seats, put her jacket on another, and plonked herself on the seat by the window.

"Jeez, what's the rush?" Freya moaned. She and her overstuffed backpack nearly got stuck in the compartment door.

"Where are the others?" Charlie asked.

"Coming," Freya answered, She hauled her rucksack into the luggage rack.

"Put your jacket on that empty seat there," Charlie said. "And pull the curtains. Don't want anyone else to come in here."

A few boys from their class squeezed through the corridor outside their compartment. Fred stuck his tongue out at Freya. Baz and Steve tried to outdo each other in being cross-eyed.

"Look at those idiots." Freya giggled. She made her most horrible face and looked back at them, squinty-eyed. Then she pulled the curtains. The boy hammered against their window once more before scrambling into the neighboring compartment.

"Right," Freya dropped back into her seat. "All the *Pygmies* are next door. Except for Willie, but he'll probably show up soon."

"And isn't that just going to be great?" Charlie muttered. She put her long legs on the seat opposite.

Someone opened the compartment door. Melanie, also known as Pretty Mel, poked her head through the curtain. "How about it? Still have space for two *Wild Chicks*?"

"Come right in!" Charlie said. "Do you have Trudie with you?"

"Of course." Melanie nudged a huge travel bag through the door.

"Morning," Trudie mumbled sleepily.

"Holy cow!" Charlie helped Melanie haul the massive bag into the luggage rack. "What have you got in there? Your entire makeup table, or what?"

"Haha!" Melanie sat down next to Freya and flicked the blonde curls out of her face. "Clothes, of course. You never know what kind of weather we might be getting."

Charlie shrugged. "As long as you have your necklace with you."

"What do you think?" Melanie was polishing her patent leather shoes. Around her neck hung a chain with a chicken feather. The same as the others, only that they had their feathers on leather bands.

The feather around their necks was their gang badge, and

only a real *Wild Chick* could wear it.

"I think we're off," Trudie said.

The train lurched into motion. It slowly inched out of the gloomy station and into the sunlight.

"Perfect weather for our little island holiday, don't you think?" Melanie produced a bag of gummy bears from her jacket and offered it to the others. "Here's to a great school trip."

Charlie and Freya helped themselves, but Trudie shook her head. "No, thanks. I'm on a diet."

"Since when?" Charlie asked.

"Since two days ago." Embarrassed, Trudie tugged at her ponytail. "I already lost a pound. Or nearly."

"A diet on a school trip?" Melanie snickered. "Not a bad idea, what with the food they'll probably be serving us."

"Exactly." Charlie looked out of the window and wrote her name on the dusty glass with her finger. The train rolled over a railway bridge. Beneath them the filthy river glittered in the sunlight. "You know what? I'm quite excited now."

"Really? Just yesterday you were trying to convince us to play sick so we could all stay home," Freya said.

"Yes—yesterday?" Charlie replied. "Yesterday was yesterday."

Next door, the *Pygmies* were singing soccer songs.

"Totally untalented," Melanie observed. "What do you say? Should we sing something as well?"

Charlie groaned. "Oh no! Please spare us."

"Melanie has a good voice," Trudie said. "She's in the choir. First soprano." Trudie was Melanie's biggest fan. She adored her, twenty-four seven.

"Great!" Charlie screwed up her face in disdain. "But if she starts singing here, then I'll jump out of the window."

Melanie had just opened her mouth to retort with a not-so-friendly comment when there was a knock on the compartment door.

"The conductor!" Trudie whispered. "God, where did I put my ticket?"

But it was only Baz, the smallest and loudest member of the *Pygmies*.

"Hello to the poultry club!" he screamed. "Here's a message for you."

He threw a rolled-up piece of paper into Freya's lap. Then he made a curtsy and slammed the door shut again.

"Oh!" Melanie screwed her eyes. "I bet it's a love letter. Baz is after Freya again."

"Rubbish!" Freya muttered. But her face was bright red.

"He also wrote love letters to Melanie once!" Trudie whispered importantly.

"Well, that was ages ago," said Charlie. "Come on, Freya, read it."

Reluctantly, Freya unrolled the paper. The other chicks eagerly leaned forward.

"No love letter," Charlie announced. "That's Fred's scrawl."
Fred was the chief of the *Pygmies*.

"'Warning to the Wild Chics,'" Freya read. "God! He can't even write 'chicks' properly. Why don't they just call themselves The Dyslexics?"

"What's the warning?" Trudie asked. She adjusted her glasses uneasily.

"Hold on," Freya smoothed the paper, "It's not easy to decipher this. 'We, the infamous Pygmies, hereby *anounce* that the piece *treety* with the stupid Wild Chics is not valid in other places. So be on your *gard*, Chics! Signed: The Pygmies." Freya lifted her head. "Oh no, not all that again!"

"I knew it!" Charlie called out. She rubbed her hands. "Wonderful. Oh, they're going to regret this!"

"But the treaty is still valid on the ship, isn't it?" Trudie asked. The mere thought of the ferry that was to bring them to the island made her face go quite green. "I don't want them to steal my sick bags. I get awfully seasick."

Charlie shrugged. "That's an important detail. I'll clear that with Fred."

"Those ferries really don't roll that much," Freya said.

"And anyway…" Melanie snickered, "It'll do wonders for your diet."

Trudie just managed a tortured smile.

CHAPTER 2

Trudie got seasick. Even though that day the sea really was quite peaceful, and the old ferry they were on did not roll at all.

But Trudie was not alone. Mrs. Rose, their teacher, also kept disappearing to the toilets and Steve, the *Pygmies'* resident magician, could not complete a single card trick. His face soon turned as green as the linoleum on the cafeteria floor.

And while Trudie spent the crossing in the smelly head, Melanie hung out with Fred and Baz by the slot machines. Considering their suspended peace treaty, Charlie found that kind of behavior quite inexcusable, but she wasn't in the mood to get angry. Instead, she joined Freya up on deck. They looked at the sea and let the salty air blow in their faces, and they generally felt wonderful. Freya was glad to be getting away from home for a few days. Since her mother was working again, she'd had to look after her little brother even more often than before. And Charlie—Charlie thought there couldn't be anything better than to be leaning on a ship's rails, her best friend by her side, and looking out over the sea. And Freya was definitely her best friend.

"Wouldn't be too bad, being a gull like that, right?" Freya said. "I think I'd like that."

"But then you have to eat raw fish all day." Charlie leaned over the rusty guardrail and spat down into the gray waves. "I think I'd rather be a pirate. On a big sailing ship, with the sails above me, rattling in the wind, the ropes creaking. I'd sleep in the crow's nest every night, until I know all the stars by heart."

"Doesn't sound too bad either," Freya sighed. She squinted into the sun. "Look there, dead ahead. I think that's our island."

From the ferry they got on a bus and, by the time they pulled up in front of the youth hostel, it was already early afternoon.

Mrs. Rose's legs were still a little wobbly from the crossing, but she still managed to get her whole class gathered around her. Mr. Dustman, English teacher and 'male escort' on this trip, was standing a little off to the side, looking rather bored, as usual.

"Right!" Mrs. Rose's voice still sounded a little shaky after the crossing. "Our rooms are on the first floor, on the corridor to the right. No pushing, no shoving. There's a bed for everyone. You can now take your things up to your room in a calm and orderly fashion, and then we'll meet down in the entrance hall at four for a little stroll on the beach. Agreed?"

"Beach stroll!" Baz screwed his eyes. "Sounds killer exciting."

Mrs. Rose just gave him one quick glance and he immediately fell silent. She was quite good at that.

"What about food?" Steve asked anxiously. His face had returned to its normal pinkish hue.

"Lunch is at one o'clock sharp," said Mrs. Rose. "So we won't get any today. That's why you were all supposed to pack a lunch."

"I already ate that," Steve said miserably.

"And barfed it out again!" Fred added with a broad grin.

"Well, you're not going to starve to death, Steve," Willie growled. "Your flab reserves should last you until dinner."

Steve blushed, and Mrs. Rose clapped her hands.

"Well then," she said, "Off to your rooms, you lot. Mr. Dustman and I will do an inspection round later on."

"Come on!" Charlie hissed at the other *Chicks*. "The first room is ours."

They ran as fast as they could, which, thanks to Melanie's huge bag, wasn't very fast. Trudie helped her carry it, but they still got overtaken on the stairs by a lot of kids. By the time the *Chicks* got to the corridor, the first room was already taken. The next one also already had two boys in it.

Fighting for breath, Charlie stormed into the third room. "Damn! Six beds!" she yelled. "Do these all have six beds?"

Freya and Melanie came in and looked around.

"Well, I'm sleeping in the top bunk," Melanie said. "I can't breathe in the bottom one."

"I'm taking that one." Charlie dragged her bag to the top bunk by the window. "Okay?"

"I don't care," said Freya. She put her rucksack on the bunk under Charlie's.

"Where's Trudie?" Charlie asked nervously. A couple of kids had already put their heads through the door, but no one had yet come in to claim a bed.

"Trudie's bag broke open," said Melanie. She plopped a chewing gum between her brilliant white teeth. "Right on the stairs. She had to get all her things together."

"What? And you just left her there?" said Freya. "After she helped you with your huge bag?"

"I had to take my own bag to the room first!" Melanie said indignantly.

"I'll help her!" Freya ran to the door.

"And how am I going to block all these beds?" Charlie shouted after her.

"You'll manage," Freya answered. And then she was gone.

Melanie and Charlie looked at each other.

"Don't look at me!" Melanie hissed. "Now it's all my fault again, or what?"

The door opened again. Three girls from their class peered inside.

"Have you got any beds left?" one of them asked shyly. Her name was Wilma. Next to her was Matilda, who was new in their class.

"Of course they're free," said Nora, the third girl. She pushed her way past the others into the room.

"No, they're not," Angrily, Charlie planted herself in Nora's path. "Freya and Trudie are still coming."

"And?" Nora threw her bag on to the free upper bunk. "That leaves two beds. Even a chicken brain can see that."

Charlie pursed her lips. Melanie said nothing. She was again polishing her shoes.

"Hi!" Freya pulled a panting Trudie into the room.

"You see?" Charlie folded her arms. "Those two belong to us. One of you has to go."

Wilma and Matilda looked at each other. "I'm not leaving," said Wilma. "The only other bed is next door, and that's with the bitches. I'm not going in there."

"Well, my sympathies, but one of you will have to stay with them." Charlie quickly took Trudie's bag and threw it on the bunk beneath Melanie's, who was sitting up there brushing her hair.

"I could go," she said. "I don't mind."

"Are you crazy?" Charlie looked at her, dumbfounded. "We swore to stay together. Have you forgotten that already?"

"Swore? Oh dear!" Nora pulled a face. She produced a comic book from her bag and settled with it on her bed.

"Of course, the four of you are a gang. Crazy Ducks or something."

Charlie shot an angry glance at her.

Wilma and Matilda were still standing in the door.

"It's okay. I'll go," Matilda murmured.

Without another glance at the other girls, she dragged her bag back out into the hall. Then she quietly shut the door behind her.

Freya gave Charlie a withering look. "Couldn't you've been a little nicer? She's all alone. And now she has to go and stay with the bitches and listen to their endless talk of boys and clothes."

"They're really not that bad," said Melanie.

"Really?" Charlie looked at her angrily. "Well you certainly seemed keen enough to get over there."

"Stop fighting!" Trudie shouted. She had tears in her eyes. Trudie was very prone to tears.

Wilma put her bag on the bunk beneath Nora's and sat down next to it. She was smiling happily.

"You know what?" She bounced up and down on her mattress excitedly. "I was hoping I'd end up in your room. I want to be a *Wild Chick* as well."

Charlie frowned. "Do you now? Well, it's not possible. Four is enough. And anyway…" she rubbed her nose, "…you'd have to survive at least one adventure before you can become a *Wild Chick*. A test, you know?"

"What test?" Trudie asked, baffled. "I never did…"

Charlie shot her a warning glance, and Trudie quickly shut her mouth.

"I tell you what, Wilma." Melanie jumped down from her bunk. "Being a *Wild Chick* is really not that great anyway."

Charlie looked as if she was going to explode any moment.

"Although," Melanie continued, "We do have a lot of fun. A lot of fun! For example, when we catch fish."

"Fish?" Wilma was puzzled.

"*Pygmy*-fish," Melanie explained.

The other *Wild Chicks* grinned. Oh yes, they all remembered that adventure. And the *Pygmies* were probably not going to forget it either. As long as they lived. Quite amazing that they had dared to break the peace treaty after that defeat.

"Where have the *Pygmies* gotten to anyway?" Charlie asked.

"We could check," said Freya. "How are you feeling, Trudie?"

"Oh, since the floor stopped moving, I'm quite okay," Trudie answered.

Wilma jumped up from her bed. "Can I come with you?"

"No!" said Charlie. She opened the door.

Melanie poked her head through the door. "Nothing happening out there," she reported. "I can only smell Dustman's cigarettes."

"Then let's go!" Charlie whispered.

As quietly as field mice, the *Wild Chicks* crept into the hall.

Nora didn't stir from behind her comic book, but Wilma looked after them full of envy.

CHAPTER 3

The *Pygmies* were in a four-bed room at the end of the corridor, right by the washrooms. Finding them turned out not to be that difficult, for they had left their door wide open, and Baz's voice could be heard all the way down the corridor. He was once more telling jokes only he could laugh about.

And Freya. Freya was the only one in their class who laughed about Baz's jokes. Just as she did now.

"Stop giggling!" Charlie whispered as they tiptoed toward the open door.

"Sorry!" Freya whispered, but she immediately started again.

"Right, you better stay here, then," Charlie hissed. "You and Trudie—find out where the teachers' rooms are. Melanie, you're with me."

The two moved on, soundlessly, until they stood in front of the *Pygmies'* open door.

"Hey, check this out," Steve was just announcing, "I have a new trick."

"Seen that one already, Steve," said Fred. "Willie, close the door. Time for a *Chicks* conference."

"Right." Steps came toward the door. Melanie and Charlie

pressed against the wall as close as they could.

"Hold on," they heard Willie say. "I can smell…" With one big leap he was in the corridor. "Hello, Melanie," he said with his best Frankenstein grin. "I knew I recognized that perfume. Hey Fred, check out who's here."

"Don't get all smug!" Charlie pretended as if she was looking straight through them. "We were just going to the washrooms."

"Is that right? Well, you walked right past them," Fred replied. "Maybe you should call yourselves the Blind Chicks."

"You know what we do with spies?" Willie asked.

"Nope. What's that?" Melanie blew a chewing gum bubble and let it burst right in front of Willie's nose. You had to give it to her—she was not the timid type. Even though everyone knew that Willie did not have an iota of humor.

"If you weren't a girl," Willie growled, "I'd…"

"Leave it," Fred pulled him back.

Melanie just linked arms with Charlie, gave the boys another big smile, and vanished with her friend into the washroom.

"Jeez, Melanie!" Charlie pulled her arm free. "Do you have to cover yourself with that perfume all the time? Now we still have no idea what they're planning."

Melanie shrugged. She was looking in the mirror. "And? Kind of makes it more interesting, don't you think?"

She pulled a little brush from her pocket and started

brushing her hair. Charlie was dumbfounded.

"What happened?" Trudie came panting into the washroom. "We saw them catch you."

Charlie nodded. "Because Melanie likes to smell like a flower on legs. All we know is where their room is."

"The teachers' rooms are by the stairs," Trudie said. "Right at the beginning of the corridor. You can already see the smoke coming out from under Dustman's door. And Mrs. Rose hung her name plate on the door handle."

Melanie was done brushing. "Where is Freya?" she asked.

"She wanted to check where Matilda ended up. She feels bad about the thing with the room."

"Tell her to get me the baby monitor," Charlie said. "Right away."

"What baby monitor?" Melanie asked.

"I told Freya to bring her little brother's baby monitor," Charlie answered. "As soon as the boys go downstairs, I'll sneak into their room and hide the thing there. You just have to make sure they don't come back up again."

"Mrs. Rose will take care of that," Trudie said. "But what's the baby monitor for?"

"So we can listen to the *Pygmies*," Charlie explained. "The sound isn't great, but it'll do. Freya and I tried it out at home."

Melanie grinned. "Not bad." She looked at her watch. "We have to be downstairs in ten minutes. Don't be late. You know how Mrs. Rose hates that."

Charlie nodded. "No problem. Just get Freya here."

Barely a minute later, Charlie heard someone rush down the corridor.

She jumped off the window ledge where she had settled herself halfway comfortably—and froze.

"Hi Freya," she heard Baz say. It sounded as if he were standing right in the washroom door.

"Hi!" Freya answered a little breathlessly.

"How, eh…" Baz cleared his throat, "…how's your room?"

Charlie put her ear on the door. *What was this now?*

"Good," said Freya. "We can see the sea."

"Great." Baz again. "We have no view. I like the sea. You too?"

"Eh, yes. A lot," said Freya.

Charlie looked at her watch. Nearly four. How long were those two going to be chatting out there?

"What that funny thing in your hand there?"

Damn. The baby monitor. This was getting dicey. Freya was a useless liar.

"That? Oh that." Freya started stuttering. "That's, eh, that's the charger for—for my electric toothbrush."

"Weird," said Baz. "Well, see ya, okay? I'll buy you an ice cream."

"Okay," Freya said.

Then she escaped into the washroom. Charlie was nearly knocked out by the door.

"What the hell was that?" she hissed. "I've been standing here so long my feet are as flat as pancakes."

"There." Freya put the baby monitor by one of the sinks. "What was I supposed to do?"

"Charger for an electric toothbrush?" Charlie giggled. "Not bad. But now get downstairs. Tell Mrs. Rose I'm still on the toilet."

"Right. See ya," said Freya. And she was gone.

And Charlie waited for the *Pygmies* to also make their way downstairs.

CHAPTER 4

The weather was still perfect as Mrs. Rose led the whole class down to the beach. Mr. Dustman was bringing up the rear. Every now and then, he cast a bored glance at the sea.

Charlie's little delay had earned her a reprimand from Mrs. Rose, but it didn't seem to have roused any suspicions with the *Pygmies*. Charlie had found a wonderful socket for the baby monitor right next to Fred's bed. And now it was waiting there, hidden behind a curtain, for its first deployment. Charlie could hardly wait.

"Beautiful, isn't it?" Freya nearly stumbled over her own feet because she kept looking out at the sea.

"Hmm? Yeah, great," Trudie muttered. She was unhappily nibbling on an apple while, a few steps ahead, Steve emptied a whole bag of chips.

Melanie also didn't look too happy. "One thing that's really annoying about the seaside is that blasted wind!" she moaned. "Feels like it blows right into one ear and out through the other."

"Put on a cap," Charlie said. "You won't look perfect, but your ears will stay warm."

Melanie ignored that remark.

"Hey, Charlie!" Someone behind her was tugging her

sleeve. It was Wilma. "Look what I made." She proudly held out a string with a feather on it.

Charlie squinted at it angrily. "Hey, only real *Wild Chicks* are allowed to wear one of those. Take that off!"

That stung. Wilma quickly tucked the feather back under her jumper.

"I won't!" she said. "And it's only a gull's feather anyway, and you can't stop me from wearing one of those, can you?"

Freya grinned, and Trudie had to chuckle. Charlie shot them both an angry look.

Wilma tucked at her sleeve again. "Hey, Charlie! How about it? Should I spy a little for you? Or keep watch? You can never have enough look-outs."

"No!" Annoyed, Charlie tried to speed up, but Wilma kept up with her, even though Charlie's legs were nearly double the length of Wilma's. The others were still giggling.

"Forget about it!" Charlie hissed. "Our gang is full."

Wilma looked around and lowered her voice. "I could spy on the *Pygmies*," she whispered. "They won't suspect me."

"She's got a point," Melanie said.

"Yes, exactly!" Trudie tried to throw the core of her apple into the sea, but instead it hit Steve on the back of his head. She quickly ducked. Steve looked around, but he couldn't spot anyone suspicious.

"I've already sorted the spying," Charlie growled. "I have…"

"Let her try," Freya interrupted her. "Those baby monitors

crackle a lot and the boys could quite easily spot it."

"Fine!" Charlie shrugged. "But that doesn't mean you're part of the gang."

"Oh, thanks!" Wilma whispered. "Super great! I'll get to work right away."

She looked around. Willie and Baz had rolled up their trousers to their knees and were splashing around in the icy cold water, trying to get anyone wet who came into their range. Hardly any secret information to be spied out there. So Wilma glued herself to Fred's heel. He was collecting shells and stones, stuffing his haul into Steve's backpack. Wilma had to be careful not to run him over.

"Look at her!" Melanie giggled. "Wilma, our secret weapon."

"I think I'll check on Matilda," Freya said. She stomped off through the sand to the new girl, who was walking the beach all by herself. Baz immediately stopped chasing Willie across the beach, and started sauntering toward the two girls.

"Ah!" Melanie nudged Charlie. "I was right, after all! He's after Freya. Probably because she's the only one who laughs about his stupid jokes."

"Maybe he just wants to sound her out, about our plans."

"Charlie!" Melanie rolled her eyes. "You really are clueless. You still think everyone takes that gang crap as seriously as you do."

"Why crap?" Charlie looked angrily at Melanie. "You're having fun with it as well, right?"

"Of course," Melanie brushed the tousled locks from her face. "But that," she pointed at Baz and Freya, "Is something else. You want to bet? Let's make it two packs of chewing gum. Tomorrow she'll have a love letter from him."

"Okay. You're on." Charlie bent down and picked up a shell. They were really quite pretty. "What's with that Nora anyway?" she asked.

"Oh, she kind of hangs out with the other two who had to stay down (*repeat the class*)," said Trudie.

Charlie nodded. She looked out at the sea with a gloomy face. "The boys are lucky," she mumbled. "They have a room to themselves. And we're stuck with Wilma and Nora. Can't even hold a proper gang meeting there."

"Of course we can. Wilma is totally your fan, and Nora…" Melanie picked up a few pebbles and threw them into the water. "Nora doesn't care about any of our stuff anyway. To her we're all just a bunch of stupid babies she's now stuck with."

"Hmm," Charlie grumbled. She'd still rather have a room with just four beds.

They'd already been trudging through the wet sands for ages when Dustman caught up with Mrs. Rose in giant steps and, smiling, held his watch under her nose, convincing her that it was finally time to head back. The sun hung low over the ocean. The tide was going out, and the water shrunk away from the beach like a large slouching animal.

"I was beginning to think Rosey was going to have us walk

all the way to the horizon!" Trudie groaned. "I can barely lift my feet. And I am so hungry! Drives me crazy. I hope it's not going to be like this every day."

"Oh, there'll be lots of walking," Melanie said. "Beach walks, night walks, dune walks…"

Trudie sighed.

The Pygmies also seemed to have grown quite tired. They were trotting along the beach listlessly, together with Titus and Bernie, the two biggest posers in their class.

Wilma gave up her spying and re-joined the *Wild Chicks*. Very inconspicuously, of course. She crouched down between Charlie and Melanie and pretended she had to tie her laces.

"Titus the bore is telling some story about his diving adventures," she whispered. "He's already escaped three killer-sharks. And before he got started, they just talked about soccer. Maybe that's some kind of secret code. They kept using strange abbreviations, like UEFA, AFC and stuff. Maybe that means something?"

"Nope." Melanie plopped another chewing gum into her mouth. "Those are all about soccer."

"Sure?" Charlie asked.

Melanie grinned. "Definitely."

"Bummer," Wilma muttered. She looked crestfallen. "I could try again."

"No, leave it," said Charlie. "We're nearly back at the hostel anyway." She looked around.

Freya was walking with Matilda a few feet away. Charlie was actually a bit jealous. Just a tiny bit.

It was nearly six when they returned to the hostel. Dinner time. After dinner, Mrs. Rose assembled them all at the bottom of the stairs again.

"The rest of the day is yours," she announced. "The games room, with the table soccer and the ping-pong, will be open until nine. At nine o'clock sharp, you will all be back in your rooms, please. Mr. Dustman and I will be checking up on you. Lights out at eleven. Breakfast is at seven thirty."

"Seven thirty?" Steve cried out. "I thought this is a holiday!"

"Seven thirty," Mrs. Rose repeated. "We'll wake you at seven. That will be Mr. Dustman's job."

Mr. Dustman smiled as he produced a whistle and held it up in the air.

"Furthermore," Mrs. Rose continued, "No flooding of the washrooms, no sneaking along the corridors after eleven, and no, I repeat, no excursions to the beach without one of us teachers. Clear?"

"Clear," the class muttered back.

"Oh," Mr. Dustman cleared his throat, "And please no toothpaste under the door handles of the teachers' bedrooms. That's really way too infantile."

"We could always use sunscreen," Baz said.

The others snickered. Mr. Dustman only rolled his eyes.

CHAPTER 5

The *Pygmies* played foosball. From six until nine. Without a break. They also devoured immense amounts of chips, screamed 'goal!' all the time, and gave each other silly names, such as Crouch, or Rooney—and they generally pretended as if the *Wild Chicks* did not exist.

Charlie was deeply insulted, but Melanie, Trudie, and Freya were quite happy and they thought they should have a cozy evening on their room, with tea and biscuits. Only Wilma understood Charlie's disappointment. She suggested to at least put a few of the mushy bananas from dinner in the boys' beds. Charlie was quite taken with that idea.

But, just as they had managed to convince the other three to pay a little visit to the Pygmies' room, Steve had himself substituted off the foosball table so that he could practice some magic tricks up in their room.

"Blast!" Charlie muttered as they were all sitting on their beds. Nora was still downstairs. "That idiot Steve with his stupid magic trick mania. You know what he's trying to do right now? He's trying to make a ball disappear in a towel. It's just that he keeps dropping it to the floor."

"Oh, stop being such a grouch." Melanie looked around. "Where did you put the tea tins?"

"By the window." Charlie was the tea expert.

"Vanilla, Rose Leaf," Melanie read out, "Tropical Fire, Cornish Blend. What do you want?"

"Cornish," Freya suggested. "That sounds cozy."

The baby monitor crackled. Steve must have dropped his ball again. They heard him cursing under his breath.

"That thing is really great," said Trudie.

Melanie shook some tea into the tea egg and hung it into the teapot Charlie had brought along. Then she went off to the teachers' tea kitchen. Camping cookers were sadly not allowed in the rooms.

While she was gone, Trudie put five big mugs on the only table in the room. Five. Wilma beamed.

After a whole eternity, Melanie finally returned. "Couldn't get it done any faster," she said, putting the steaming teapot on the table. "Mrs. Rose was there before me, and you know who else was there? Pauline, that old swot. 'Mrs. Rose, I also want to be a teacher one day. Mrs. Rose, math really is my favorite subject. My participation in class has improved, hasn't it, Mrs. Rose?' I thought I was getting the measles from just listening to her."

"Yes, Pauline is hard to take. Here," Freya threw a few paper sachets on the table, "I got two sugars from dinner."

Melanie took the tea egg out of the pot and carefully distributed the tea and the sugar into the five mugs. Finally she handed one mug to each *Chick*, including Wilma, who pressed the warm mug against her cheek. "Oh, this is so cozy!" she sighed. "A gang really is the coziest thing in the world."

Charlie shot her a dark look. "That's actually not what a gang is about." She grumpily stirred her tea. "If Steve's going to be practicing his tricks again tomorrow, then we have to find a way to lure him out of that room. We actually might try that right now, what do you think?"

"Oh, come on!" Melanie dug into her bag. She produced a tin of cookies and put it on the table. "This is our first evening here. Just forget about the boys for once. You saw for yourself—looks as if they have forgotten about us."

"Exactly," said Trudie. "It's actually quite wonderful here. I'm not at all homesick. What about you all?"

Melanie and Wilma shook their heads.

"Homesick? What, like for my gran?" Charlie slurped her tea and looked out of the window. "No, definitely not."

Charlie spent a lot of time at her gran's because her mother drove a taxi. Charlie's gran was not what you would call a friendly person, though she had taught Charlie a lot about teas, and vegetables, and real chickens.

"I only miss my little brother," Freya said, "Because he's so wonderfully cuddly just before bedtime. But apart from that it's really nice here."

"I just hope," Melanie climbed into her bed, "That none of you snore."

Trudie blushed, but she said nothing.

"Listen!" Wilma suddenly whispered.

It was just before nine.

The baby monitor crackled briefly, but there was someone in the corridor. The wooden floor creaked treacherously. The *Wild Chicks* stared at the door with bated breath. The handle moved. But Charlie had locked the door.

"Hey, open up!" someone whispered. "It's me, Nora. Why did you lock the door?"

Charlie leaped off her bed and ran in socks to the door.

"Hi Nora, your voice sounds awfully scratchy," she said.

"I drank too much tea," the strange voice answered from outside. "Can you open up now?"

"Fred? Is that you?" Melanie called down from her bed. "Is your voice finally breaking?"

Loud cackles from outside.

"We're having chicken fricassee tomorrow!" Willie shouted.

"My money is on *Pygmy* roast!" Charlie called through the keyhole—and she immediately got a load of water in her face.

More loud cackles from outside.

"Nothing like a little night-time refreshment!" Steve called.

"Hey Steve, give me that water pistol," Willie said.

Then they heard Nora's real voice. "Would you idiots let me through, please? Yuck, put that water pistol away." Nora rattled at the door. "Open up. Now!"

"Can't do that," Wilma answered meekly. "The *Pygmies* will just come in here."

"If you're talking about the bunch of shrink heads who were just hanging around here—Mrs. Rose and Mr. Dustman are coming up the stairs and now your friends have all disappeared."

"They are not our friends!" Charlie unlocked the door. "They are the *Pygmies*."

"Yep, sounds about right, looking at their sizes." She climbed into her bed and grabbed one of her comic books.

"Do you want tea?" Trudie asked.

"Nope, thanks!" Nora answered. "What's that infernal noise?"

"Oh, the baby monitor!" The *Wild Chicks* quickly gathered around the small speaker.

"And, Steve? Did the *Chicks* try anything?" They heard Fred ask. Then there was a terrible crackle and a bang.

"If they're going to lock their door every evening, we'll have to try in the daytime to…" Another loud bang.

"Hey, Baz!" Willie yelled. "Stop that hopping around, okay? Your mattress is already knocking against my head here." Another crackle. "How far did you get with Freya?"

Trudie giggled.

Freya jumped up and yanked the monitor out of the socket. "Enough!" she said. "This really is too stupid. Bugging other people's rooms. Disgusting!"

She flung the monitor into her bag and lay down on her bed.

"This whole gang thing," Nora said from behind her comic book, "Really is idiotic."

"That's none of your business!" Charlie hissed. A gloomy silence fell over the room.

Another knock on the door.

"Everything alright in here?" Mrs. Rose asked, poking her head around the door.

The girls nodded.

Mrs. Rose looked skeptical. "Not the best of moods in here, is it?"

"We'll sort it out," said Melanie.

"Fine." Mrs. Rose shrugged. "If not, or if anyone gets homesick or has any other ailments, my door is the one with the monster sticker. Some admirer must have stuck that there. Mr. Dustman will blow his whistle just before eleven, so you won't forget to brush your teeth. Have a good night. You'll see, the seaside air makes you quite tired."

"Good night," the girls mumbled.

And then they were alone again.

Melanie, Trudie, Wilma, and Charlie played cards until eleven. Freya stayed on her bed, with her back turned to them, reading a book. The *Pygmies* came to the door three more times. Once they even started poking around the lock with something. But after Mr. Dustman caught them and escorted them back to their room, the girls were finally left in peace.

CHAPTER 6

That first night, Charlie couldn't sleep. She sat up on her bed, clutching the stuffed chicken which came everywhere with her, and looked out at the sea.

Charlie's mum always said she couldn't sleep when the moon was too bright. But that wasn't it.

Everything was strange. The smell of the bedding, the hard mattress, the way the bed squeaked whenever she moved. Charlie listened to the calm breathing of the others, and to the rush of the sea. Yes, even the sounds were strange. Very strange.

"You can't sleep either?"

That was Trudie. She looked different without her glasses.

Charlie shook her head. "You want to come up?" she asked. "It's a great view from up here."

"I'd love to." Trudie felt around for her glasses, then she snuck past the sleeping Freya and climbed clumsily up into Charlie's bed.

She looked funny in her pink pajamas.

"You have a stuffed animal?" she whispered.

"Of course!" Charlie gently tickled her stuffed hen's neck. "This one goes everywhere with me. My mum gave it to me for my tenth birthday."

"I took one as well," said Trudie. "But I didn't dare to unpack it. I thought the others would make fun of me."

"Why? Melanie also has her stupid Barbie doll," Charlie replied. "And Freya has one of her little brother's jumpers under her pillow."

"Really?"

"Sure." Charlie pulled the duvet over her knees.

"But my teddy wouldn't help either." Trudie sighed. She wrapped her arms around her knees and looked out of the window. "I just can't sleep. Can't get my head quiet. Have to think all the time."

"Why?" Charlie asked. "What about?"

Trudie brushed a strand of hair from her face. "My parents are getting divorced."

"Oh!" Charlie said. That could never happen to her. She didn't even have a father.

"They fight every day," Trudie told her. "And sometimes even at night. They fight about everything, and then my dad comes in and screams at me that I eat too much and what the hell do I look like anyway. And so my mum screams at my dad again, and then they send me to my aunt's for a few days, so they can continue to fight in peace."

"Sounds horrible!" Charlie mumbled. She didn't know what else to say.

"How does it feel?" Trudie anxiously looked at Charlie. Her glasses were all fogged-up. "I mean, with only a mother.

What's that like?"

"Fine." Charlie shrugged. "It's fine with just my mum around. Only that she has to work so much. But, you know, that's just the way it is."

"Hmm." Trudie looked at her toes.

That had sounded quite sad. Charlie would have loved to cheer her up, but she couldn't think of anything. So they sat there in silence, side by side on Charlie's bed, and looked at the sea, on which the moon had laid a silver varnish.

They sat like that for quite a while.

Finally, Trudie got cold and snuck back into her own bed. But not before she had fetched her teddy from her bag. It was a white bear, and it wore pink pajamas, just like Trudie.

CHAPTER 7

The next morning, everybody seemed a little bleary. The thin red tea they got for breakfast did nothing to wake them up and, when Mr. Dustman announced a nice long walk to the next village, the general mood sank below freezing point.

"What's with the long faces?" he asked. "We'll actually be coming past two very interesting prehistoric burial mounds."

"Oh, I know the kind!" Fred groaned. "They just look like humps in ground. Very exciting."

"Mrs. Rose won't be coming with us," Mr. Dustman continued. "She is a little indisposed this morning."

"I am indisposed, too!" Baz called out with a high-pitched voice. "Can I stay as well?"

Mr. Dustman ignored him.

Fred had been right about the burial mounds. No skeletons, no mummies, no treasure—just two humps in a meadow. Mr. Dustman did tell them a story about the rumor that a tribe of elves lived in those mounds, but they were also nowhere to be seen. Instead, the boys got on everyone's nerves with their water pistols, brand new PowerShot 2000s, that had annoyingly large water tanks. Only when Maximilian, also known as Minimax, drenched Mr. Dustman's cigarettes, were they all ordered to empty their weapons out on the burial mounds. And when it then started to rain as well, the mood in the class turned riotous. Even Wilma had lost her usual enthusiasm.

"And? What do you think of these Friesian houses?" Mr. Dustman asked as they finally entered the small village which he had declared their destination. Thatched cottages ducked under yew trees, one next to the other.

"Nice," Trudie mumbled.

"Not bad," said Wilma, picking her nose. "Is there anything else to see here?"

"Well, not much, but we are here for a reason." Mr. Dustman made his important you'll-see-soon-enough face, which he usually put on when he returned graded homework.

"Tell us!" Someone called.

But Mr. Dustman shook his head. "Only one of your classmates might be able to guess, but the rest of you will have to remain in…distress. Ah!" Mr. Dustman turned around. "That was actually a rhyme. Follow me, ladies and gentlemen."

Grumbling and groaning, the whole class fell in behind him.

"What's that supposed to mean: one of us could guess it?" Melanie's brow had deep furrows.

Trudie and Wilma shrugged.

"The houses are really quite pretty," Freya said. "Very nice.

And the gardens have so many flowers!"

"Yes, not at all like my gran's, right?" Charlie linked arms with Freya. "Are you still upset about yesterday?" Freya shook her head.

"Would you…" Charlie rubbed her nose, "I mean, could you imagine giving us the monitor back?"

Freya pulled her arm away like lightning. "You are incredible!" she called. "Impossible!"

"We can always switch it off, whenever," Charlie started to stutter, "Whenever there's something about love or stuff."

Freya just left her standing.

"Damn!" Charlie muttered. She saw Baz pick some flowers that were hanging over one of the fences and run after Freya. "That hopeless lard-brain."

"She won't give it back, will she?" Wilma asked.

"Are you now spying after us as well?" Charlie barked at her.

"No!" Wilma replied crossly. "Is it my fault when you talk so loudly?"

Charlie's face darkened. She was furiously chewing her lip.

The street with the old houses led them to the harbor, where some fishing boats and excursion boats were bobbing on the dark water. Screeching gulls were picking garbage off the waves. Mr. Dustman led the class past some souvenir shops and finally stopped in front of a café.

"Right. Ladies? Gentlemen?" he called. "Now it is time to reveal the true purpose of this dreadful march. Matilda, would you please come to me?"

Matilda turned as red as a tomato. Hesitantly, she went to stand by the teacher's side.

"It is Matilda's birthday today!" Mr. Dustman announced. "And, knowing you—and her—my guess is, nobody knew that. And I think a birthday calls for a certain celebration. And that is why I am inviting you all to join me in Matilda's honor in this café. For a hot chocolate, or a Coke, whatever you like. I, for one, will indulge in an Irish coffee."

During Mr. Dustman's short speech, Matilda was looking down at her hands, but she was smiling.

In the café, they pushed three big tables together. Dustman placed himself and Matilda at the top end. He made the whole class sing Happy Birthday—during which he thankfully only conducted—and then he ordered a round of drinks, ten hot chocolates and seventeen Cokes. Then he happily slurped his Irish coffee and read his newspaper.

For a while, the boys flicked paper pellets across the table and bombarded the girls with sugar cubes. Then they all descended on the only slot machine by the entrance of the café. Wilma, the tireless spy, inconspicuously skulked around near them, while Freya invited Matilda to a piece of chocolate cake. Together with two other girls, they retreated to a table by the window. Freya had Baz's flower tucked behind her ear.

And soon there were only Charlie, Trudie, and Melanie left behind with Mr. Dustman. Trudie yawned constantly, while Charlie thought hard about what she could put in the *Pygmies'* beds. Melanie was painting her toenails. Then Mr. Dustman suddenly appeared from behind his newspaper.

"Oh, by the way, did anyone notice anything strange last night?" he asked. His voice sounded a little bored, as usual. "I'm not talking about your little gang tiffs. Anything unusual? Inexplicable noises, maybe a scratch on the door? Lights on the beach? No?"

"Why?" Charlie looked at him with surprise.

"Oh," Mr. Dustman reached for his mug. "I just thought. You—eh—kind of hear about things."

"What things?" Trudie forgot her yawning.

"Nothing special. Something about the ghost of a long-dead beach master." Dustman looked at them over the rim of his mug. "He's supposed to be doing his haunting right by our hostel. Sounds rather farfetched, don't you think?"

"A ghost?" Wilma called out. "A real ghost? Jeez!"

Even the boys at the slot machine turned around.

"Shh!" Charlie hissed. "They don't all have to know about it!" She turned back to Mr. Dustman.

"What kind of a ghost?"

"Really, there is no such thing as ghosts," Melanie said, before she resumed blowing on her freshly painted toenails.

"A colleague told me about this one." Mr. Dustman lit one

of his hideously stinky cigarettes. "He was here last year, with his class. And supposedly some strange things happened."

"What things?" Trudie asked anxiously.

Mr. Dustman shrugged. "Unpleasant sounds in the night. Strange footprints and mysterious objects on the beach. There were two students who ran screaming from their room one night, jabbering about some horrible something that wanted to drag them into the sea. I don't know more than that." He tugged his earlobe. "But why am I telling you that? You probably have more than enough on your plate with those *Pygmies*."

"Those?" Charlie waved dismissively. "We would have stopped that childish stuff long ago, but they keep starting it again. No, tell us more about the haunting...what was he again?"

"A beach master," said Mr. Dustman.

"What is that?" Melanie asked.

"A beach master is a kind of guardian of the beach." Mr. Dustman signalled the waitress for another Irish coffee.

"Whenever a ship sank by this island, the beach master had to make sure that the cargo wasn't plundered. However, the beach master who's been haunting this island for more than two hundred years is supposed to have been quite a plunderer himself. His name was Lap Jornsen and the people here," Dustman stirred his coffee, "Still tell stories about his heinous crimes."

"What did he do?" Wilma whispered.

"Well," Mr. Dustman shook his head, "They are quite horrible. I'm not sure."

"We're not babies anymore!" Melanie said indignantly.

"You're right about that. So..." Mr. Dustman stopped and took a long, slow-motion slurp from his coffee mug.

"So?" Charlie asked impatiently. Dustman really could be quite annoying sometimes.

"I can only tell you what I heard," he said, carefully dabbing his lips with his napkin. "And if you get nightmares from this, don't tell me I didn't warn you."

CHAPTER 8

"Lap Jornsen was a strange beach master," Mr. Dustman continued. "Every poor farmer who stole a beached butter barrel because his children were starving, he'd have flogged and thrown into jail. But he never raised a finger to help castaways. No, he would let them drown slowly, so that he could grab the cargo of their ship without witnesses."

"Yuck!" Wilma muttered. "Someone like that of course has to turn into a ghost."

"You think?" Mr. Dustman looked amused. "It gets worse. There was nothing particularly unusual about Jornsen not rescuing any castaways. Back then, nobody was particularly inclined to risk their own neck for a strange castaway whose language they might not even understand. And a little bit of plundering, yes, but Lap Jornsen went quite a devilish bit further." Mr. Dustman reached for another cigarette. "Whenever there was a storm out at sea, he'd let his men light fake signal fires, luring the ships onto the sands off the island, where his men would plunder them. And any seaman who didn't drown in the icy waves he had killed, so that nobody could tell about his crimes."

Dustman leaned back with a sigh. "That just leaves us the

hope that his ghost is a little nicer than the man was when he was alive, right?"

"Was he never caught?" Melanie asked.

Dustman shook his head. "He was far too powerful for that. Oh, and by the way!" He brushed some ash from his jumper. "This afternoon you'll see his picture in the island museum. And his gravestone in the old cemetery, which we will also visit." Dustman lowered his voice. "It's supposed to be standing askew, because Jornsen never found rest in his grave."

"Uuugh!" Wilma shuddered. "That sounds pretty spooky."

"He just got away?" Charlie muttered. "That's hideous!"

"He just died in peace, probably very old and filthy rich," Melanie said. "Did he?"

"No quite," Mr. Dustman answered. "You could say he met some kind of justice. He was poisoned, shortly before his fifty-fifth birthday, by the widow of a captain whose ship sank because of his fake signals."

"No!" Trudie's eyes went wide. "How horrible."

"Why? Served him right!" Melanie nodded, satisfied. "I would have done the same." She put another layer of green paint on one of her toenails.

"I can imagine that someone like that turns into a ghost!" Charlie mumbled pensively. "Just a pity that there are no ghosts."

"What are you all huddled up for?" Baz asked curiously.

He sat down at the table.

"None of your business!" Charlie replied. "You just go back to your slot machine."

"So, you didn't notice anything, then?" Mr. Dustman's face again looked quite bored. He took another drag from his cigarette. "No suspicious sounds, footprints, objects on the beach? Old coins or something? Supposedly Jornsen keeps dropping some on his nightly haunting excursions."

The girls shook their heads.

"What do you mean?" Baz asked. "Strange noises? Jornsen? Haunting?"

Damn. Charlie angrily bit her lips. Now the *Pygmies* would also learn about this.

"Oh, we just had a little chat about our hostel's resident ghost." Dustman stubbed out his cigarette and picked up his newspaper. "I just wanted to check whether anyone noticed anything strange between, say, ten and eleven o'clock last night. But it seems our ghost is on vacation."

"A ghost? Jeez!" Baz was getting all jittery with excitement. "Tell me about it!"

"Find out for yourself," Charlie retorted tetchily.

"I will," Baz shot back. "You can bet your beak on that, you stupid hen."

"Now, now!" Mr. Dustman said from behind his newspaper. "No hostile acts in my presence, please. The short version is that there's supposed to be a two-hundred-year-old ghost in our hostel, someone who already was quite a nasty character when he was alive. The rest I'll tell you on our way back."

"All right!" Baz jumped up. "I have to tell the others about this. This is way more exciting than water and stupid graves with nothing inside."

He quickly ran off to the others. Soon the *Pygmies* were sitting at a table in the deepest corner of the café, whispering intently. They didn't even notice Wilma, who had placed herself at the neighboring table.

"Do you think the story is true?" Trudie whispered. "I always wanted to meet a ghost. This one sounds quite nasty, though."

"It is definitely harmless," said Melanie, "Because there's no such thing as ghosts."

Trudie chewed her fingernails. "I'm not so sure about that."

"Yes, because you keep watching these silly movies," Melanie taunted her. She leaned back and looked over toward the boys.

"So, it can't be a ghost, that's for sure. But maybe…" Charlie rubbed her nose, like she always did when she was thinking, "…maybe someone is haunting the hostel because he's buried something hideous somewhere, and now he wants to make sure that nobody starts digging around the beach."

"What is it?" Trudie asked breathlessly.

Charlie replied with a meaningful shrug.

Trudie's nose turned white. "God! How horrible."

"Nah, you want to know what I think?" Melanie said. "If there's someone playing a ghost, then it's to attract more tourists."

"You think?" Trudie looked disappointed. "That would be a really boring story."

"I already thought of that," Mr. Dustman said from behind his paper. "But why the hostel? Very few tourists ever come that way, except for the very rich ones."

"Exactly!" Charlie sighed with relief. "It can't be that."

"Maybe it's aliens?" Trudie lowered her voice. "They do exist, you know. My father saw a UFO, right above our balcony."

"Another very interesting subject," said Mr. Dustman, laying his newspaper aside. "But I'm afraid," he glanced at his watch, "We now have to quickly get back, on the double, or else we miss lunch."

CHAPTER 9

They nearly did miss lunch. Mr. Dustman led them back to the hostel at a murderous pace. Freya stayed with Matilda the whole way, Wilma eavesdropped on the *Pygmies*, and Trudie, Melanie, and Charlie discussed Dustman's story. There wasn't much time, because after Dustman had told the *Pygmies* all the details of Lap Jornsen's story, he had the class sing shanties non-stop. "My Bonnie went over the ocean…" and "When the Alabama's keel was laid, roll Alabama, roll…"

It was quite horrid.

Hoarse and out of breath, they all piled into the dining hall and quickly dispersed on to the remaining empty tables. Charlie, Melanie, and Trudie sat at one table. Freya shot Charlie a dark look before she sat down with Matilda at another table. But of course Wilma squeezed herself between the *Wild Chicks*.

"I've got something!" she panted. "I heard something. Two, in fact!"

"Two what?" Charlie asked.

"Secrets! Top quality," Wilma hissed.

Charlie looked around, but the *Pygmies* were sitting far away. And they were anyway fighting with the boys at their neighboring table. The *Pygmies* shouted: "Gunners!" and the others retorted with: "Man U!"—whatever that was supposed to mean. Then Willie had the idea to catapult potato mash at them, and Mr. Dustman immediately intervened, allotting 'voluntary' kitchen duty to Fred and Willie and two of the other boys.

Charlie turned back to Wilma. "Shoot."

"There's a ghost," Wilma panted. "In the hostel."

"We know," Melanie said.

"Oh!" Wilma was crestfallen. "How did you know that?"

"Dustman told us," Trudie explained.

"Yes, and Baz heard it as well," Charlie growled.

"Do you also know that the *Pygmies* are planning to catch the ghost?" Wilma hissed.

Charlie frowned. "Really? How?"

Wilma shrugged apologetically. "They want to plan the details tonight."

"Damn!" Charlie helped herself to some more mashed potato, even though it was so gooey that stuck to her teeth. "We don't have the baby monitor. Freya won't give it back. Just because that idiot Baz is making pretty eyes at her."

"Who cares?" said Melanie. "Let them try to catch their ghost, which doesn't even exist. We might as well try and catch the Loch Ness monster. Yum, that cabbage isn't half bad."

"What monster?" Trudie asked. She had only taken a tiny

portion. Melanie was already devouring her second helping.

"And what was the second secret?" Charlie asked. She looked around once more. Fred, Willie, and Baz were done with their lunch, but Steve was shovelling another helping onto his plate.

"They put something on our pillows," Wilma whispered. "During breakfast, while Steve and Willie said they had to go to the bathroom. Itchy-bitchy, they called it. Steve got it in some shop where he buys his magic stuff."

"Itching powder! They have itching powder." Melanie shuddered. "Yuck, that's really mean. And they know that Trudie is allergic to a ton of things."

"I'm itching just from thinking about it!" Trudie whispered.

"They'll pay for that," Charlie hissed. "After all, pillows can be swapped, right?"

Trudie and Melanie nudged each other and giggled.

"Wilma!" Melanie appreciatively patted their spy on the shoulder. "I think you make a great *Wild Chick*."

"Oh, thanks!" Wilma smiled sheepishly. She looked at Charlie, who pretended to be busy with her food.

"Charlie!" Trudie leaned over the table. "What do you say? Shouldn't we let Wilma swear the *Wild Chick* oath? Tonight. Sort of as a reward, I mean!"

But Charlie frowned. "This is a bit quick, isn't it?"

Wilma disappointedly poked at her mashed potato.

"Nonsense!" Melanie pushed her plate aside and attacked her desert. Trudie looked longingly at the pudding. "Why make the poor thing wait? I say she becomes a *Wild Chick* tonight!"

"Agreed!" said Trudie. "And Freya," she looked over toward her, "Freya probably agrees as well."

Melanie grinned triumphantly at Charlie. "You've been overruled!"

"Fine!" Charlie grumbled. "Whatever. Thanks to her we don't have to scratch ourselves all night. The spying thing really was quite a good idea."

"A good idea?" Fred was suddenly standing behind Charlie, putting his chin on her shoulder. "Hens never have good ideas."

Charlie shoved him away. "Buzz off!" she said. "Your head is just full of soccer and nothing else."

"We'll catch the ghost before you!" Steve announced. His voice squeaked with excitement. "I'll bet you anything."

"Oh, the ghost." Charlie made a bored face. "You can have it. We're a little too old to believe in ghosts."

"Duh! As if we believe in ghosts!" Fred said huffily. "Or do you think we're stupid enough to buy stuff like that? You know what?" Fred leaned toward Charlie until his nose nearly touched hers. "You're just trying to get out of our bet. I bet you anything you like that we'll find out first what's behind that ghost story."

"That's stupid!" said Melanie. "What's there to find out? There's nothing behind it."

But Charlie stared at Fred. She was chewing her lip, and finally she said: "You're on. We bet you whatever you like."

"A dance for each of us with the *Chick* of our choice." Baz called out.

Willie did not look very enthusiastic, but Fred and Steve grinned.

"Good idea, Baz!" said Fred. "And? Do we have a bet?"

Charlie shrugged. "If that's what you want. Since we're going to win anyway…"

"And if we win," Wilma interrupted. "Then you have to carry our bags, on the whole trip back."

"Deal," Fred nodded. "But since when are you a *Wild Chick*?"

Startled, Wilma pursed her lips. The *Wild Chicks'* spy had blown her own cover.

"She isn't," said Charlie. "But the idea is good. The bet is on."

The *Wild Chicks* and the *Pygmies* shook hands on their wager.

"And what about Freya?" Baz asked. "Isn't she with you anymore, or what?"

"Of course she is," Charlie shot him her most withering look. After all, it was this shortie's fault that she was fighting with her best friend. "She's also going to stick to our deal."

"Promise?" Baz looked over at Freya.

"Promise," said Charlie.

Now she only had to sell the idea to Freya.

CHAPTER 10

Wilma came panting up the stairs. "They're playing foosball again!" She really was a first rate spy. "They've got a whole tournament going, with Titus, Bernie, and the twins."

"All of them?" Charlie asked.

"It's always two against two, but they keep swapping places." Wilma grinned. "They are all totally into it."

Charlie gave a satisfied nod. "Then let's go."

They dashed to their room. Nora wasn't there. She was downstairs, writing postcards. But Freya was sitting by the window, looking out at the ocean. When the others came storming in, she spun around. "What's happened now?"

"The *Pygmies* put itching powder on our pillows," Trudie said. "And now we're swapping our pillows with theirs."

"Itching powder?" Freya wrinkled her nose. "Yuck!"

Charlie tried a cautious smile. "Will you help us?"

Freya hesitated for a brief moment. Then she shrugged. "Sure."

Carefully, very carefully, the *Wild Chicks* picked up their pillows and carried them to the door. Wilma held it open. Then she quickly followed them with her pillow. It was quite a procession.

"And what do we have here?" Mr. Dustman was smoking a cigarette by the open hall window.

"We, ehm…" Charlie couldn't for the life of her think of a good excuse.

"Never mind," Dustman put the cigarette in his mouth again. "Forget I asked."

Then he turned back to the window.

The five girls quickly moved on.

On the door to the *Pygmies'* room was a piece of paper with a clumsily drawn skull.

"Is that supposed to make us run for our lives?" Melanie asked.

"You know, I think," Charlie put her ear against the door, "The skull doesn't look half as bad as your green fingernails."

"Ha-ha!" Melanie poked her tongue at Charlie.

"And? Can you hear anything?" Trudie whispered.

"Nope, but wait a minute," Charlie bent down. "Check this out. Not so dim-witted after all, those guys. We should do something like that as well."

"What is it?" The others peered over her shoulder.

"They stuck a piece of paper down here on the door," Charlie said, carefully removing the sticky note. "If we'd just walked in there, the paper would have been torn off and they would have known. But, dumb as they are, they made it too big. I spotted it when I was listening."

She balanced her pillow on one hand, opened the door

with the other, and quickly slipped inside. The others followed. They swapped the pillows as quickly as they could.

"Who should I give my pillow to?" Wilma asked. "Mine is kind of extra."

"Give it to Fred," Charlie replied. "He loves playing the boss, so he gets two pillows." She looked around. "I can't believe it. They even put up soccer posters."

"And a flag." Astounded, Wilma approached the huge thing. "What country is that?"

"That some soccer club." Melanie screwed her face up. "Ridiculous."

"Well, you've got posters of some weird pop-star on your wall," said Freya. "Kind of the same, isn't it?"

Trudie giggled. "The mouth on one of her posters is all smudgy from her kisses."

"Shut up!" Melanie hissed at her. Her face had turned all red and blotchy.

"Okay!" Charlie tiptoed back to the door. "Let's get out of here."

They scurried back out into the corridor. Charlie carefully replaced the piece of paper, then the whole pillow procession marched back down the corridor. Dustman shook his head as he looked after them.

CHAPTER 11

They at least took a bus to get to the museum. Clouds had appeared during lunch, and it started raining as soon as they left the hostel. The clouds hung dark over the island.

"Bummer. We probably won't even get to swim once!" Melanie sighed.

"Suits me," said Charlie. She didn't particularly like water. Most of all she hated being ducked under, which was a speciality of the *Pygmies*.

The first thing they saw as they climbed out of the bus was a huge arch made from the jawbone of a whale. It was a memorial to the times when the people of the island had lived mainly off whaling. Behind the white bones was the large thatched building that housed the museum.

"Yuck!" Baz shouted out as he stood between the bleached pillars of the strange arch. "I hate walking through the bones of a murdered singing fish."

"Whales aren't fish," said Wilma, shoving him along.

"Duh, I know!" Baz pulled a face at her. "Because they don't lay eggs. And? They still look like fish, right?"

"You know what?" said Mrs. Rose, putting her arm around his shoulder. "That's exactly why I got into trouble with my biology teacher. I still think whales are fish."

"As if they care what we think they are," Willie grumbled. "As long as we leave them in peace."

Baz looked up at Mrs. Rose in surprise. "You had a biology teacher?"

"A horrible one," Mrs. Rose whispered to him. "A complete creep."

Waiting for them by the entrance was a small round man with mutton chop whiskers and a fisherman's shirt. He looked with obvious disapproval at the approaching unruly group.

"Can we have some quiet, please?" Mrs. Rose called out. "This here is Mr. Applecurd, who has kindly agreed to give us a tour of the museum. And of course there are a few rules. No touching…" Mr. Applecurd nodded his round head vigorously. "…Don't tip anything over, and, above all, pay attention."

"The last rule in particular," Mr. Dustman added with a raised voice, "You should heed particularly well because, once we get back to school, you will have the pleasure of writing an essay about this museum."

General moaning ensued.

Mr. Applecurd smiled gleefully.

There was actually a lot to be seen in the small museum: traditional dresses, weapons from the time of the Vikings, stuffed sea birds, and a real captain's cabin. The exhibits from the days when nearly the whole island engaged in whaling were particularly creepy. The harpoons, blubber knives, and huge paintings made them all shudder. But apart from that, everyone saw something they found interesting. Melanie spent a lot of time by the old jewelry and festive folk costumes, while Steve was caught feeling the breasts of a wooden figurehead. Mr. Applecurd was incensed.

The last room was filled with portraits of captains and their families, mayors, parsons, and—Lap Jornsen, the beach master who had doubled as a raider.

"That's him!" Wilma whispered to Charlie. "Did you imagine him like that?"

"No!" Charlie shook her head. "He looks harmless. Probably wouldn't have made such a great ghost after all."

The *Wild Chicks* and the *Pygmies* scrambled to get as close as possible to the painting.

"He doesn't look at all like a murderer," Freya mumbled. The others had briefed her during the bus ride about Mr. Dustman's story and the terms of the bet with the *Pygmies*. She had not liked those at all.

"No, Lap Jornsen did indeed not look like a criminal," Mr. Applecurd announced. "That was probably also how he managed to maintain a double life for so long—as a brigand *and* a pillar of the island's community."

"Is it true that he's a ghost now?" Fred called out.

Mr. Applecurd exchanged an amused glance with Dustman. "That is indeed what people say. Some claim that's the reason why his gravestone by the church is so crooked."

"Disgusting!" Steve whispered. He looked apprehensively at Lap Jornsen's clear blue eyes.

"And what does he do?" Willie asked. "I mean, when he's out haunting."

"Oh, the story goes that he moans and groans and scratches at walls," Mr. Applecurd informed them. He cast a satisfied glance at the children, who were suddenly all quiet and attentive. It was obviously rare for him to have such a rapt audience. "He also leaves wet footprints. And when he's been haunting the beach where he killed all those poor sailors, we usually find a few coins in the sand, as if he were trying to pay for his sins." Mr. Applecurd rocked back and forth on his feet. "That is what the legend tells us. The legend," he turned to face the gloomy portrait of the beach master, "Of Lap Jornsen, the most terrible beach brigand this island has ever known. And there have been many!" Mr. Applecurd looked at the children crowding around him. "Any questions?"

"Is there a painting of the woman?" Melanie asked. "The one who poisoned him?"

Mr. Applecurd shook his head regretfully. "We sadly don't have one. But we do know a few things about her. Her name, for example. She was called Frederika Mungard, and she did not have the money to have herself painted. A portrait was quite a luxury in those days."

"Bummer," Trudie whispered.

"What happened to her?" Charlie asked.

"What do you think?" Baz grabbed his own throat. "Krrk, executed."

"Oh no." Mr. Applecurd shook his head. "After the deed she disappeared, together with her four children. Some fishermen probably took her to the neighboring islands, or to the mainland. Some say the half the island aided her escape."

"How romantic!" Wilma sighed.

"Not really," said Mr. Applecurd. "And the rest of her life probably wasn't that romantic either. She was a widow, with four children. No money. No property. No, definitely not very romantic. But I believe," Mr. Applecurd cast a quizzical look at Mr. Dustman, "That is enough about this part of the exhibition. I suggest we now turn our attention to the whalers."

"Another bunch of criminals," Fred muttered.

But Mr. Applecurd hadn't heard that.

They returned from the museum in time for dinner. After dinner, it was already dark, but Charlie still managed to convince Mr. Dustman to accompany them to the beach for a while. While he sat in the dunes and smoked cigarettes, the *Wild Chicks* scoured the beach with their torches, looking for Lap Jornsen's coins. Soon the *Pygmies* turned up as well, of course. Fred had wrangled a shovel from the hostel's caretaker, and they immediately started digging through the sand.

Charlie eyed the boys suspiciously. "At least Fred and

Willie are on kitchen duty tomorrow."

"I hope they don't find anything," Wilma breathed.

So far, the girls had only found a few crabs, seashells, and a couple of empty beer cans.

"I've got something!" Trudie suddenly called out. "I found a coin. There!"

The *Pygmies* dropped their shovel and stared over at them.

Melanie pointed her torch at Trudie's find. "That's just a ten cent piece," she said.

The *Pygmies* went back to work, looking relieved and hooting taunts at the girls. But they had also not found anything yet, as far as anyone could tell in the darkness. After half an hour, the girls lost interest. They were frozen stiff and their clothes were damp from the sea air. Even their lips tasted salty. The boys had also abandoned their digging. They were huddled together in the sand. The *Wild Chicks* dropped into the sand and looked gloomily at the ocean. Only Freya was still cheerful.

"I would sit here forever," she mumbled. "It's so beautiful. If you close your eyes, the rush of the waves goes right through you."

Trudie closed her eyes. "You're right," she said. "I can feel it way down in my belly."

"Well, my bum's frozen stiff," said Melanie. "I'm going back. This is stupid anyway."

Mr. Dustman came stalking over from the dunes. "Enough

for today?" he asked.

"Yes." Charlie scrambled to her feet. "Stupid idea, to go digging around here in the dark."

"There!" Trudie shouted. She reached into the sand, just a hand's breadth from Dustman's shoes.

"What, there?" Melanie sighed. "Another ten cent piece? Come on, let's go inside. I need a cup of hot, hot tea."

"No, look!" Trudie called. "There. Those look quite old."

Incredulous, the others leaned over her sandy hand. The *Pygmies* jumped up and came closer. Trudie had found three large, crusty coins. They had a crest on one side, and the number ten on the other.

"Look, Mr. Dustman," Freya said.

Mr. Dustman took the coins from Trudie's hand and studied them closely. "Yes, these have not been in use for a long time," he confirmed. "I'm not an expert, but this could indeed be some of Lap Jornsen's blood money."

He put the coins back in Trudie's hand, and she quickly closed the fingers around her find.

"Hey, Trudie. You better lock your door tonight," said Fred. "Everybody knows ghosts always come to get their money back."

"Yes, exactly!" Baz shouted. "But of course locking the door won't do you any good. Good old Lap can just stick his bony hand through the wall next to your bed."

"Stop it!" Charlie shouted angrily. "You're just jealous! You didn't find anything."

Trudie was nervously chewing her lip. She pushed the hand with the coins deep into her pocket.

"Come on, Trudie." Charlie pulled her along. "Just don't listen to those jerks."

The *Wild Chicks* followed Mr. Dustman through the dunes. The bright windows of the hostel were quite a welcome sight after the darkness on the beach.

"Huuuuu!" The *Pygmies* howled behind them. "Haaaaaargh! Toooooooniiiiiiight weeee graaaahaaaab little rooooound Trudie!"

"You mean little shits!" Wilma shouted back, throwing handfuls of wet sand at them. "You miserable little wieners!"

"Ignore them!" Charlie whispered to Trudie. "They're just mean because they're jealous."

"Exactly!" Melanie linked her arm with Trudie's. "But soon," she lowered her voice so that Dustman couldn't hear them, "They'll be scratching themselves anyway, and they won't be able to think of anything else."

"I don't care what they say!" Trudie said, snivveling just a little. "But I still would like one of you to take the coins. Since you all don't believe in ghosts anyway."

The other *Chicks* looked at each other. None of them reached out to take them.

"Give them to me!" Freya said finally. "I'm only afraid of live criminals. And that guy's definitely not alive anymore."

74

CHAPTER 12

After they had brushed their teeth, the *Wild Chicks* locked their door. Charlie even wedged a chair under the handle. Nora was lying on her bed, poking fun at their paranoia, but the *Wild Chicks* ignored her. They were preparing for Wilma's formal swearing-in as a *Wild Chick*. Melanie announced that the room needed to be made more festive for the occasion, and she hung her pink silk scarf in front of the window. She even tried to tie a bow on Charlie's stuffed hen, but Charlie quickly put a stop to that. Freya made some rose leaf tea, and Trudie lit some of the candles they had brought along. Wilma fetched the mugs. She was so excited that she dropped one, but luckily it did not break.

"You think the *Pygmies* already have their heads on their pillows?" Charlie suddenly asked.

"They're probably waiting for us to lie down," Melanie said. "Which means they'll be waiting for a while."

They all sat around the table.

"Could we turn off the light for a bit, Nora?" Freya asked.

"What for?"

"To make it look more festive!" Trudie answered. "Wilma will have to swear the oath in a minute."

A loud groan from Nora's bed. "God! You are such a bunch

of babies! Five minutes, and not a second more."

The big bare room immediately looked cozier in the candlelight.

"Right!" Charlie said. "Wilma, do you still want to be a *Wild Chick*?"

Wilma breathed: "Yes!"

"Then stand up and repeat after me…"

Wilma jumped to her feet so quickly, she nearly spilled her tea.

"I swear…" Charlie began.

"I swear…" Wilma repeated.

"…to protect the secrets of the *Wild Chicks*…" Melanie continued.

"…to protect the secrets of the *Wild Chicks*…" Wilma breathed.

Trudie took over: "…with my life, and never to tell anyone anything."

Wilma repeated: "…with my life, and never to tell anyone anything."

"Or I will happily drop totally dead on the spot." Freya said.

Wilma swallowed hard. "Or I will, erm, happily drop totally dead on the spot."

Nora chuckled. She thought this was all very amusing.

"What's totally dead?" she asked. "Is there also a little dead?"

"Oh, shut up!" Charlie said angrily. "Spit on your fingers. You too, Wilma."

The five girls spat on their index fingers, then they rubbed them all together.

"Done!" said Charlie. "Now we are five."

"Strength in numbers!" Melanie carefully wiped her finger with a tissue. "Five to four. Those *Pygmies* won't know what hit them!" She gave Wilma a nudge. "How do you feel? Now that you're a real *Wild Chick*?"

"Wonderful," Wilma whispered.

"Now all you need is a chicken feather," Freya said. "Charlie can get you one from her gran's chicken coop."

"That won't happen any time soon," Charlie grumbled. "My gran and my mum aren't speaking—again. We'll have to make do with a gull's feather for now."

"Lights!" Nora shouted. "I want to read! Damn, why is this so itchy all of a sudden? Did you have a cat in here? I'm allergic to cats!"

"Oh no!" Trudie giggled. "You know what? We completely forgot her pillow!"

"Yes!" Freya and Melanie were giggling, too. They couldn't stop themselves.

"What do you mean?" Nora roared. "You forgot my pillow? Forgot what with my pillow?"

"The *Pygmies* put itching powder on the pillows," Charlie explained, grinning broadly. They switched the lights on. "We took ours over to their room. But we forgot yours."

"Itching powder?" Nora was frantically scratching her head and neck. "I can't believe it. I really can't believe this!" She jumped out of her bed and ran to the little sink in the corner.

"What's it feel like?" Wilma asked. "Itching powder?"

Nora just gave her a murderously angry look. "Damn. I'll have to wash my hair as well," she muttered. "Just because of your baby pranks."

"I can give you a great shampoo!" Melanie said with an angelic smile.

Nora didn't even look at her.

"I wonder what's happening in the boys' room." Charlie listened at the door. "I can't hear anything. Great, then we can have another look at Trudie's coins."

"There." Freya put them on the table.

Trudie eyed them with owner's pride—and with a little unease. "They look quite real, don't they?"

Melanie frowned. With her green fingernails, she scraped some of the sand from the notched metal. "And? That still doesn't mean that they were dropped by Jornsen. I still think this is all a tourist-gimmick."

"Still, I'll be sitting by the window tonight, keeping an eye on the beach," Charlie said. "But first," she walked to the door, "I'll check on the *Pygmies*. Don't want to miss them all scratching themselves like a bunch of flea-ridden monkeys. I'd never forgive myself." She pushed the chair aside and unlocked the door. "Anyone coming?"

"Me!" Wilma said.

Nora was wrapping a towel around her wet head. "I hope they roast you," she hissed. "As you do with stupid chickens."

Trudie grabbed Charlie's sleeve. "Why don't you stay? I mean, because of the ghost and that."

"Rubbish!" Charlie slipped through the door with Wilma in tow. "It's much too early for ghosts. Lock the door behind us and don't let anyone in. Understood?"

"Understood!" Melanie said, closing the door behind them.

The corridor was pitch dark. Only a tiny bit of light came from under the doors. They could hear laughter from the other rooms, and somewhere someone was bouncing on a squeaky bed. Mrs. Rose's room was silent, but there was a dim band of light coming from under her door. Mr. Dustman's room was dark.

"Should we turn on the light?" Wilma whispered.

"Why not? We could just say we needed to go to the toilet." Charlie flipped the switch, but nothing happened.

"Weird," she muttered. "Did you bring your flashlight?"

"No, I left it behind," Wilma whispered.

"Never mind," Charlie whispered back. "Let's go."

She carefully tiptoed ahead. She heard loud splashing from the washrooms. And curses. Angry curses. *Pygmy* curses.

"Listen to that!" Charlie giggled. "The gentlemen are already under the shower. Trying to wash off their own stuff.

Another victory for the *Wild Chicks!*"

"That's what you think!" someone growled behind her.

Wilma uttered a little high-pitched shriek. Charlie spun around in surprise. Someone grabbed her and covered her mouth. She knew that grip. That could only be Willie. Fred had Wilma in a chokehold, which was probably much more pleasant.

"Willie and I had a little pillow fight," said Fred. "That's probably why our scalps aren't itching right now, right?"

Charlie angrily squinted at him. She couldn't say anything because of Willie's iron hand on her mouth. She tried to bite into it, but not even that worked.

Wilma looked at her miserably over Fred's hand. Charlie tried to stomp on Willie's feet, but she couldn't reach them. Willie was simply too experienced in holding prisoners.

"Let's go, Willster—to their room," Fred whispered. "But watch out—Rosey lives opposite to them. You have our little present?"

Willie nodded.

Yes, Mrs. Rose. Charlie had just been about to reach for Willie's hair. But if Mrs. Rose found out about their little gang war, they'd all be in trouble. Big trouble. Mrs. Rose did not like gangs—at all.

And so Charlie let herself be dragged to the *Chicks'* room. Wilma wriggled and kicked, but Fred did not let go of her.

"Hey, you, in there!" He knocked on the door three times.

"Open up!"

For a few moments there was silence. Then they heard something rustling behind the door.

"No way!" Melanie answered.

"I'd say: way!" Fred said quietly.

"We have Charlie and Wilma!" Willie hissed through the keyhole. "And we'll tickle them until you open up."

That did it for Charlie. Never mind what Mrs. Rose would say. She would not be a hostage. Never.

She yanked one arm free of Willie's grip, grabbed a handful of his hair, and pulled at it with all her strength. Backwards. Willie squealed like a pig. For one startled second he loosened his grip, and that was all Charlie needed. As quick as lightning, she freed herself. An angry Willie was nothing you wanted to be close to, and angry was exactly what he was. His faces contorted with rage as he tried to shove Charlie against the wall, but she ducked and jumped on Fred to help Wilma.

That very moment the door opened.

Charlie couldn't believe it.

Nora was standing in the doorway, her towel still wrapped around her head. "I've had it up to here!" she screeched. "Quit that babying around right now!"

Melanie pushed in beside her and blocked the door. Her rage painted bright red blotches on her face. "We didn't want to open," she panted. "But that stupid cow was too quick."

She shot Fred an angry glance. "Let go of them. You're not coming in here, even with your secret helper here!"

Nora stuck her tongue out at Melanie.

Fred grinned. "We don't want to come in," he said. "We just wanted to leave a little gift."

Willie quickly pulled something from his pocket and threw it at his boss—and Fred threw it over Nora's wrapped head into the room.

Charlie knew immediately what it was.

And to make the whole disaster complete, Mrs. Rose was now also coming down the corridor. "*Wild Chicks* and *Pygmies*," she shouted. "Of course! I thought you had buried the hatchet? What…" Mrs. Rose sniffed and her face screwed up with disgust. "A stink bomb? Have you gone mad? Do you know that we could get kicked out of here for that? There is something like house rules, you know!"

"It was just a joke!" Fred mumbled. He didn't even dare to look at Mrs. Rose.

"A joke?" she said sharply. "Maybe I should make a little joke and call your parents. Hmm? Who threw that thing?"

Chicks and *Pygmies* stayed silent, as was the unwritten rule. But they had forgotten about Nora.

"Him!" she said, pointing at Fred. "He threw it. And now I get to sleep in this stench. And I have nothing to do with their stupid gang stuff." Her voice was trembling with rage.

"You can sleep in my room," said Mrs. Rose. "And you…"

she shook her head as she looked at the *Wild Chicks*. "I am inclined to believe you brought this onto yourselves, right? Still, the stinkbomb was thrown by the boys, and so they should enjoy the fruits of their labor. My suggestion is you all swap rooms for the night."

The *Wild Chicks* looked far from delighted.

"No, Mrs. Rose," Charlie said quickly. "We want to stay in our room. We can handle that bit of stink."

"Couldn't get a wink of sleep in their room anyway," Wilma added. "With all those soccer-heads on the walls."

"Oh?" Mrs. Rose gave her a surprised look. "Are you now also part of that crazy bunch, Wilma?"

Wilma looked at the floor.

Mrs. Rose sighed. "You heard them," she said to the *Pygmies*. "Your victims have refused compensation for tonight. But I promise you, if there is even the tiniest bit of monkey business in the evenings, I will split you up and put each one of you in a different room. Understood?"

"Yes, Mrs. Rose!" the *Chicks* and the *Pygmies* mumbled.

Mrs. Rose looked up at the light. "Is the lack of light in here also your doing?"

"We unscrewed the lightbulb," Fred breathed.

"Then I suggest you put it back in right away," Mrs. Rose said. "And I repeat: this is the last evening where anything happens between you all. Is that clear? Otherwise this trip will be over for you. You can get all your horseplay out of the way during daytime and outside. No matter what happens, I will not see your faces out here after nine."

"And what if the ghost comes?" Fred asked. "How are we going to get to it if we can't even get out of our room?"

"Oh, old Jornsen!" Mrs. Rose shook her head. "Yes, I can see how that story has made an impression on you. If that old beachcomber turns up, you can always call me or Mr. Dustman. But I think that's not very likely. And now off to bed with you."

Fred took Willie's arm and turned him around.

"This time you really blew it!" Charlie hissed at him.

"Okay, okay, I get it!" Fred grumbled.

And then he and Willie slunk off to their room.

CHAPTER 13

Freya scrubbed the place where the bomb had hit until her back ached. They opened the window was wide as possible. But the stench stayed, as if it had glued itself to the walls. The room just got cold, really cold. Staying up was simply not an option anymore.

The five of them tucked themselves into their beds, the duvets pulled up to their noses. But sleep was not an option, either.

The surf swooshed outside. Apart from that, there was silence. No more giggles from the neighboring rooms.

"Well, we really managed to ruin this evening thoroughly," Freya said into the silence. "If we keep it up, we might even ruin the whole trip with our stink-bomb-itchy-powder-whatever stuff."

"We?" Charlie held her soft chicken very close, though that didn't make her feel any warmer either. "*They* brought the itchy powder, and the stink bomb."

"I know." Freya sighed. "But we should just stop it now. They had their fun, and we had ours, and now it's all good. We only have three days left here. Or are we just going to go on like this?" She paused for a moment. "Baz also says he doesn't really like the gang war stuff anymore."

"I've had it!" Melanie said. She pushed her duvet off and climbed out of her bed. "I'm closing the window!"

"Can you see anything out there?" Trudie asked.

"Old Jornsen, you mean?" Shivering, Melanie leaned out of the window. "Oh yes, he's drifting around down there. Yuck. Gross! He looks all moldy and the skeletons of his victims are all dancing around him."

Trudie looked at her suspiciously.

"Ieeeugh," Melanie held her hand over her eyes. "Now he's pulling their bones apart and throwing them into the sea."

"No way!" Trudie muttered. But she still climbed out of her bed and tiptoed over to Melanie to peer over her shoulder.

"I knew it," she said disappointedly. "Nothing. Absolutely nothing."

"Exactly!" Melanie patted her cheek. "And you couldn't see anything anyway. You're not wearing your glasses." She slammed the window shut and turned around. Suddenly she stopped and eyed Trudie from head to toe.

"Goodness! Where did you get those pajamas?"

"Why? From my mum." Trudie looked down at herself. "My mum buys all my things."

"But you look like a huge baby!" Melanie said. "How could she buy you something like that?"

Trudie turned around without a word and crawled back into her bed, pulling the duvet up to her chin.

"Jeez, Mel! Do you have to be like that?" Charlie asked.

"We're not saying anything about your clothes either."

"And?" Melanie spun around to face her. "Should I say: 'wow, Trudie, that's a great outfit. I'd love to get that myself? Trudie, your hair looks great. Trudie, you're not at all fat.'"

Trudie sobbed audibly.

"You could also try and say nothing for once," Freya said.

"Like you, you mean?" The red blotches were back. "You all think the same, but you never say anything. You think that helps?" Melanie crouched down by Trudie's bed. "Tell you what: forget about the pajamas, but tomorrow you're getting a hair makeover. I know how to do it. My cousin showed me. She's a real hairdresser. And your mum can't do anything about it. What do you think?"

"What kind of hair?" Trudie anxiously peered over her duvet. "I'm not sure…"

That's when they all heard it.

Horrible, howling laughter on the corridor.

The five girls exchanged startled looks.

Something scratched at their door.

Charlie shot out of her bed. She reached for the doorhandle.

"No! Leave it!" Wilma whined.

But Charlie had already poked her head through the door. In a flash, all the other *Wild Chicks* were behind her.

"What do you see?" Freya asked.

The light was on, and there was at least one head poking

out of every door.

"Who was that?" asked Rita. Rita did karate, and she was definitely not afraid of ghosts.

"Might have been a cat," Paulina called from the bitches' room. Their door was only a crack open.

Mr. Dustman was also there. He was standing in his door in a bright yellow dressing gown, his hair all dishevelled. "Interesting," he said. "I'm obviously not the only one who heard some strange noises. What woke you, my dear colleague?"

Mrs. Rose came staggering sleepily out of her room. She looked totally different without her eyeliner and her red lipstick. "A very unpleasant laugh," she said. "That's what woke me. And then something scratched on my door. Poor Nora immediately hid under her bed. Honestly now—" she shot strict glances at the *Pygmies* and the *Wild Chicks*, "—was that you again?"

"No!" both gangs replied indignantly.

"It seems that, for once, they had nothing to do with this," Mr. Dustman said. "I was already out here with the last scratching sound." He shrugged. "Brightly lit, but nothing to be seen. Absolutely nothing. The doors were all shut and all the rooms were relatively quiet. Rather strange, I must say."

"The beach master!" Wilma whined.

"Told you!" Fred called out. "He wants his money back. Trudie should have left those coins on the beach."

"And what kind of a stupid ghost is that anyway?"
Baz muttered. "Comes here at eleven while we're getting
everything ready for midnight."

"Getting what ready?" Mr. Dustman asked.

"Well, stuff that needs to be ready," Fred said quickly. He
angrily shoved Baz back into the room.

"Steve, what were you getting ready?" Mrs. Rose asked.
"Spit it out!"

Steve wriggled like an eel. But Mrs. Rose's hawk-eyes were
scarier than the threat of Fred's elbows.

"Banana peels," he muttered, "For example, to make it slip
up."

The *Wild Chicks* exploded with laughter.

"Bananas!" Charlie taunted them. "For a ghost? You guys
are priceless!"

"Did you prepare anything else?" Mr Dustman asked.

Steve shrugged. "Just a bucket of water…and we put ink in
our water pistols, to make it visible."

By now the whole class was snickering.

"Steve!" Willie groaned.

"You will immediately undo all these preparations!" Mrs.
Rose said. "Or you might get the idea to use them on the
Wild Chicks. And, as far as that laughing, scratching ghost is
concerned…" she looked directly at each and every one of
them, "…if I catch him, his haunting days will be truly over."
She yawned as she turned around. "I can get very nasty," she

called over her shoulder, "If I don't get my sleep."

With that, Mrs. Rose slammed her door shut. For the last time that night.

CHAPTER 14

The third day again began with Mr. Dustman's whistle. The *Wild Chicks* groaned and pulled the duvets over their heads. On the fourth whistle, Charlie finally crawled out of her bed. She had spent half the night sitting by the window, despite the cold and the stench, while the others were peacefully sleeping. But there had not even been the pale shadow of a ghost to be spotted out there.

The room was still very smelly.

Charlie stumbled to the window and looked outside. Dark clouds hung over the sea. The sun poked through every now and then, making the water glitter as if someone had poured silver over it. But the next moment, the dark cloud shadows were back.

"No swimming today," Charlie announced, "But it's perfect weather for a graveyard visit." She yawned as she shuffled to the little sink by the window, which spared them a visit to the washrooms in the morning. That was the only good thing about their six-bed room.

"Oh, I love graveyards!" Trudie pushed her duvet aside and carefully placed her glasses onto her nose. "We sometimes go for walks on the cemetery, and we read the inscriptions on the gravestones, or look at the angels. They have beautiful angels there."

"I know! But we'll never get one of those," Melanie said. She sat at the edge of her bed and started brushing her hair. That was always the first thing she did after she woke up. "Nope, we'll just get one of those weird stones with nothing than our names on it."

"Mine is going to say…" Charlie had finished her cursory wash and she vacated the sink for Freya, "…here lies Charlotte. She had real good ideas."

"Really?" Trudie giggled.

In the corridor, the first doors were slamming. People ran around, and somewhere Mr. Dustman barked orders.

"I think graveyards are sad," said Wilma. "I'd rather have my ashes scattered over the sea. I even put that in my will."

"Will?" Freya had brushed her teeth. Now she was slowly waking up. She could never get a word out before she had brushed her teeth. "You made a will? Already?"

"Of course," Wilma said. She climbed into her jeans, brushed her fingers through her hair, and rummaged through her bag for her warmest jumper. "You never know. My aunt died when she was twenty-one. That's not that old, right? I wrote down who gets my guinea pig, so that it won't end up at the animal shelter. My books and my CDs will go to my brother. And then I also wrote down that I'd like to be scattered over the sea."

Trudie looked at her, speechless.

Melanie just shrugged. "Not a bad idea. I might do the same." She looked into her bag. "What does one wear to a graveyard?"

Charlie and Freya rolled their eyes and grinned at each other.

At that moment, the door opened. Nora entered with a gloomy expression on her face.

"I need my toothbrush," she said, not looking at any of them. "And a clean slip. Yuck!" She pinched her nose. "Still smells like a sewer in here."

Charlie looked at her icily. "And who do we have to thank for that?"

"Leave her!" Freya pulled Charlie back and went over to Nora. "We're sorry we forgot your pillow. We didn't do it on purpose. Honestly!"

Typical! Charlie rolled her eyes. Freya just couldn't stand anyone being angry with her, or if there was any kind of injustice. And in Freya's opinion, a lot of things were unjust. Much more so than Charlie.

Nora gave Freya a surprised look.

"That's okay," she finally said. "And about the stink bomb…" she fiddled uneasily with her toothbrush, "…I'm sorry about that. I had no idea those babies had such a thing."

"Oh, the *Pygmies* always have lots of stuff," said Melanie. "Stink bombs, itching powder."

"…slime, plastic spiders, plastic puke," Trudie added.

"Steve is their supplier. He always brings some along when he gets new magic supplies. It's his true passion."

"Yes, never ever shake hands with him," Melanie warned. "He sometimes has this sticky goo on his hand. It takes hours to get it off again."

"Thanks for the warning." Nora picked some underwear and two new comic books from her rucksack. She stood, hesitating, then turned around. "I'm off to the showers," she said over her shoulder. "Later."

"See you!" Freya called after her.

Once Nora had left, the *Wild Chicks* looked at each other.

"She's not so bad, is she?" Wilma said quietly.

"Nope," Freya shook her head. "Definitely no worse than us."

At least they got a break from the *Pygmies* that morning. Fred and Willie did their kitchen duty, while Steve sat at the breakfast table fidgeting with his cards with little enthusiasm. Baz was probably producing something on paper somewhere.

Later, in the bus, the boys tried to tease the girls with the stink bomb incident. But as soon as they arrived at the cemetery, Mrs. Rose confiscated all their water pistols, dampening their mood considerably.

The cemetery lay behind an old brick church, and was surrounded by high trees. It lay right in the middle between the two villages which buried their dead there. After taking a look at the inside of the church, which was not even half as exciting as the cathedral of Salisbury, they all filed out into the graveyard. Very old graves, as well as new ones, lay side by side between low hedges and neatly trimmed grass. They had no guide like Mr. Applecurd, but Mrs. Rose had brought a little book about the graveyard. She led the class over the narrow paths to the older section. Some of the graves were nearly two hundred years old. The gravestones were covered all over with ornaments and strange, swirly letters. The tops of the stones were decorated with ships, anchors, windmills, or flowery trees.

"The flowers you see there," Mrs. Rose explained, "Are family trees. Each tulip signifies a male family member, the star-shaped flowers are for the women. Snapped flowers show that a family member died before the one who is buried here."

"This one has a lot of snapped ones," said Baz.

They were standing by a gravestone showing a ship between huge waves. Next to the ship was a family tree with many flowers. Beneath them, names had been chiselled into the stone—and a long text.

"What does it say, Mrs. Rose?" Trudie asked. "Can you read it?"

Mrs. Rose shook her head. "But my smart little book probably has something about this stone. Hold on…"

"Hey, get down from there, right now!" Mr. Dustman chased Titus and Steve from the large double-gravestone on which they had settled themselves with a huge bag of chips. They jumped down and were already trampling on the next grave when Mr. Dustman took them under his arms, one to his left and the other to his right, and gave them no other choice than to listen to Mrs. Rose. She had just found the passage about the gravestone.

"This is the grave of a captain," she said. "His name was Thor Fredericks. He had sailed around the world and married four times, surviving all his wives." Fred nudged Baz and grinned. "He had seven children, but only two survived, and he died at the age of ninety-one, or, as it says here," Mrs. Rose read out loud, "He finally set sail on the black sea of death, in the hope of finding safe anchorage in the harbor of blessed eternity."

"The black sea of death," Wilma repeated.

"I wouldn't mind a gravestone like that." Fred patted the gray stone. "Looks much better than the modern ones."

"Maybe, but I wouldn't like to have a life like that," said Melanie. "Sound horrid. Nearly everyone died before him. His wives, his children. Nah!" She shook her head. "Not even the longest life can make up for that."

Mrs. Rose read some more life stories to them, about men who had made their fortune on foreign shores, and about women who lost their husbands to the ocean, or who had died giving birth to a child.

"A lot of these women died quite young," Melanie

observed, while Trudie was blissfully stroking the wings of one of the stone angels.

"No wonder, with all those babies," Charlie said.

"The children also often died quite young," Freya muttered. "Sad, isn't it?"

"And where is the grave of Lap Jornsen?" Willie asked. "That what we're really here for, right?"

"Not exactly." Mr. Dustman took a cigarette, looked at it, and put it away again. "But we could have a look around. His gravestone is supposed to be quite crooked."

They all looked around.

"There!" someone called out. "Next to those two slabs. That's the most crooked one."

The *Pygmies* jumped over a few graves and stood by the crooked stone. The *Wild Chicks* followed, but as if such childish haste was beneath them.

"That's his name!" Steve stuck a far-from-clean finger on the gravestone.

"Correct!" Mr. Dustman leaned forward. "There he is. Lap Jornsen. Born October 23rd 1740, and, as it says here so poetically, sank into death's arms September 14th 1795."

"Two hundred years ago tomorrow," Freya said.

"Exactly!" Wilma breathed. "What do you think that means?"

"What it means?" Mrs. Rose shook her head. "You really are a superstitious bunch."

"Could you read what else it says?" Trudie's eyes were wide with anticipation.

"There's not as much as on the other gravestones," Mrs. Rose said. "Here it says that Lap Jornsen was a successful merchant and a giver of alms, that he was married twice, and he was blessed with a son who erected this gravestone."

"That's it?" The *Pygmies* stared incredulously at Mrs. Rose. "And what about the murdered sailors?"

"Nothing!" Mr. Dustman produced his cigarette again, and this time he lit it, in spite of the disapproving look Mrs. Rose gave him. "It says nothing about all that, and you know why? Not even the biggest scoundrel wants to be called a scoundrel or a murderer on his own gravestone. And do you think Jornsen's son wanted to be remembered as the son of a murderer? So he made his father a nice stone. The mason chiselled whatever he was paid to do and Lap Jornsen's son could only hope that soon enough his father's crimes would be forgotten. But…" Mr. Dustman threw his half-smoked cigarette on the ground and stepped on it, "…that did not work out so well."

"And why not?" Mrs. Rose asked.

Mr. Dustman shrugged. "Stories being told on long winter nights. An old parson who could write—and soon enough everybody knew that this beautiful gravestone was nothing but a lie."

"Phew!" Mrs. Rose shuddered. "I think I've had enough

dark stories for one day." She looked at the sky. The sun was breaking through the clouds, making the grass around the gray gravestones glow bright green. Mrs, Rose held her face into the warming rays. "What do you think?" She looked at the children. "Should we get out of here?"

Nobody objected.

As they all crowded into the bus, Baz quickly pushed his way up to Freya and put a folded piece of paper in her hand. Very quickly, so that nobody would see. But Charlie saw it nevertheless.

Melanie had won her bet. Definitely.

CHAPTER 15

Lunch was great, spaghetti and tomato sauce, and three meatballs for each one of them. While they all slurped their pasta, Charlie wondered whether she should ask Freya about the note. But she didn't dare. Freya noticed that her friend was constantly looking at her. She smiled, and gave Charlie one of her meatballs. That was Freya for you. Baz really didn't deserve her. And still Charlie didn't ask her about the note. The baby monitor had taught her a valuable lesson.

When Fred and Willie cleared the plates after dessert, Trudie was called to the phone. The four others waited for her until all the tables had been cleared, but Trudie did not come back.

"Maybe she went to the toilet," Melanie suggested.

Freya shook her head. "I don't think so. Must be something to do with that call."

"No, I think she just went up to the room," Wilma said. "Right?"

"Come!" Charlie jumped up. "We'll find out for ourselves."

Mr. Dustman and Mrs. Rose were just walking up the stairs.

"Do you know who called for Trudie?" Melanie asked Mrs. Rose.

Surprised, Mrs. Rose looked at her. "Her mother. Why?" She looked around. "Where is Trudie, anyway?"

"Oh, she's probably upstairs already," Melanie said.

They quickly stormed up the last steps.

Trudie was in the room. She was lying on her bed, staring at the wall.

"Trudie?" Charlie went to her bed and sat down next to her. "What's the matter?"

Trudie snivelled. "Nothing!" she barked. But she didn't turn around.

"Would you like to be alone?" Freya asked anxiously. Trudie nodded.

Charlie got up again.

"Are you sure?" she asked quietly.

At first Trudie did not stir, but then she vigorously shook her head. She sobbed. It sounded horrible.

"Hey, hey!" Melanie sat on the edge of her bed and stroked her shoulder. "What is it? Tell us. You can talk to us."

Finally Trudie turned around. Her eyes were all puffy.

"Did somebody die?" Wilma asked with concern.

Trudie shook her head.

"My dad moved out," she mumbled. "Yesterday." She rubbed her already-red eyes.

"Wow. Your mum really could have told you after the trip," Melanie muttered. "Can't she imagine what you're feeling like now? Give me your glasses. They're all fogged up."

Trudie took off her glasses and gave them to Melanie. "She said terrible things about him," she sobbed. "And that he shouldn't dare ever to poke his head through our door again."

Melanie wiped Trudie's glasses on her skirt and put them back on her friend's nose. "Never mind!" she said. "He was only nagging you all the time anyway."

"Still!" Trudie started sobbing again.

Freya sat down on the bed and took her in her arms.

"I'll make some tea, okay?" Charlie said, feeling very self-conscious.

"Yes!" Trudie tried to smile, but it didn't really work out. "Does anyone have a tissue?"

"Sure!" Wilma quickly produced a crumpled handkerchief from her pocket. "Here. It's clean. Just looks dirty."

"Thanks!" Trudie blew her nose. For a few moments her face disappeared behind the handkerchief. "I don't ever want to go home again," she said hoarsely. "I have no idea what I'm supposed to do there. It's so much nicer here, with you guys."

"But at home we're also together," Freya said to her. "You know, as soon as we get back we have to do a lot of stuff to our headquarters, get it ready for winter."

"Right," Trudie blew her nose again.

"There." Charlie put a mug of hot tea in her hand. "I put a lot of honey in it."

"But my diet!" Trudie mumbled.

"You can forget about that for now!" Melanie said. "Go on, drink!"

Trudie obediently slurped the sweet, hot tea.

"Anyone else want some?" Charlie asked.

"Since you're asking! But only if it's Chicken tea!"

Baz and Steve.

They of course had to appear at that very moment. They were leaning in the open door, grinning. With everything going on, none of the girls had noticed the door opening. Trudie hid her puffy face in Freya's jumper.

"How about it? Steve's looking for a virgin to cut in half!" Baz called. "Any volunteers? Or are you all not virgins anymore?"

Steve ducked his head. He giggled like a kindergarten kid.

"Leave us alone, you idiots," Melanie hissed.

"Yes, off you go, play with your football machine!" Wilma added.

"Football machine!" Baz shook himself with laughter. "It's called *foosball*, you silly hen. Oh no, you're not a real hen."

"Yes, I am one now!" Wilma said proudly.

"What?" Baz fell into the doorframe with a groan. "You heard that, Steve? There's now five of them."

He shot a glance at Freya, but she wasn't paying any attention to him. She was busy with the sobbing Trudie.

"Jeez, can't you see you're intruding?" Charlie shouted at them. "Get out of here!"

"What's happened?" Steve asked.

"None of your business," Charlie hissed. "And next time you better knock, okay?"

"Oh, because you always knock?" Baz was again looking at Freya, but she frowned at him.

"You really are intruding," she said. "Okay?"

"Got the message." Baz turned around in a huff. "Come on, Steve. We have a ghost to hunt."

Charlie slammed the door shut behind them. "And you get love letters from *that*!" She said to Freya. "I can't believe it. From the biggest idiot around."

"Stop it!" Trudie blurted out. "Don't you now start fighting as well!"

Charlie bit her lip. "Sorry!" she mumbled. "Kind of just slipped out."

"I think you should apologize to Freya," Melanie said.

"Sorry!" Charlie mumbled once more. But she didn't look at Freya.

"It's not my fault that he writes me love letters!" Freya shouted. "And he's not always like that. That's just gang talk."

Charlie just looked into her mug. Her tea had gone cold.

"Charlie, Freya, Wilma!" Melanie waved them over to the window. "I think Trudie needs a distraction," she whispered. "And I already have an idea…"

CHAPTER 16

Charlie knocked on the boys' door. They were all in. Baz opened the door for her and Melanie.

"Hey, Fred!" he called. "Check out who's here."

Fred and Willie were lying on their beds, recovering from their kitchen duty. They looked at the girls with surprise.

"What's this?" Fred asked groggily. "You challenging us to a duel?"

"Charlie and I have a proposal," Melanie said.

Fred climbed out of his bed, and immediately realized that he was only wearing boxer shorts. His face went bright red as he quickly climbed into his jeans and patted down his ruffled hair. He went over to the girls.

"Right, we're listening," he said.

"Doesn't look like it," Charlie observed. Baz and Steve were nudging each other, whispering and giggling.

"You two!" Fred barked at them. "Shut up for a sec, will ya?"

Fred laid down the law. That's how it was with the *Pygmies*. It was as Charlie always said: the boys needed to have a boss. The *Wild Chicks* had none of that. Whenever Charlie said something, there were at least one or two *Chicks* who disagreed. It was annoying, sometimes, but it was still better that way.

"We're proposing a truce," Melanie continued. "Twenty-four hours. And maybe even longer."

"Why?" Willie sneered. "Are you scared that Rosey will split you up and put you in different rooms?"

"Rubbish!" Charlie hissed at him. "Trudie's parents are getting divorced, and it's really getting to her. We thought we'd have a beach picnic, to distract her a little. And your stupid itching-powder-stink-bomb attacks are the last thing we need. That's why the truce. What do you say?"

"No problem!" Baz said. "We used it all up anyway, right, Steve? Our genius magician only bought one stink bomb."

Fred looked at him angrily. "Just shut it already, okay?" He looked at the girls. "Agreed. And what about the ghost?"

"There's still tomorrow," Charlie replied. "Right now, Trudie is more important."

Fred turned to the others. "What do you think?"

"Truce," Steve chirped. "And if Trudie needs a distraction, I can always do some tricks for her."

"I'll let her know," Charlie said, turning around, but Fred grabbed her by the arm.

"Hold on," he said, "Now that we have a truce...we found something weird." He went to the wardrobe and got out... Freya's baby monitor. "Did you lose this, by any chance?" Fred asked.

Charlie tried to look anywhere but in Fred's eyes. "Possibly," she mumbled. "I could just take it back and check."

"At first we thought it's some kind of bomb," Steve said. "But then Baz told us he knows what this is. From his little sister."

"Really?" Charlie looked at Baz and bit her lip.

"I hope you heard what you wanted to hear," Fred threw the monitor toward Charlie. He grinned. "Got to give it to you, sometimes you're quite cunning, you *Wild Chicks*. Bummer we didn't think of this."

"Yeah, who knows what we might have heard!" Baz sighed.

"Yep, bummer," Charlie shrugged. "But you had some pretty cool ideas, too."

They returned the baby monitor to Freya—undamaged, and without any ransom demands. Considering they were boys, even the *Pygmies* could be quite nice sometimes.

It turned out to be a wonderful picnic.

Of course, they couldn't go to the beach by themselves. Mrs. Rose posted herself at some distance with her book. Dustman stayed in his room, for recuperation, as he put it. Whatever that was supposed to mean.

There was hardly a cloud in the sky, but the wind was still blowing quite strongly off the sea. Twice, the girls' chips bags were blown away, but both times Wilma managed to retrieve them with a heroic sprint, before they ended up in the *Pygmies'* sand castle. The boys were building with abandon, after having spent an hour looking for Jornsen's blood money.

They had found a few shreds of fabric, and Fred was totally convinced they were parts of Jornsen's burial gown. He'd put them on display on the top of their sand castle, framed by sea shells and pebbles, as if they were some sort of crown jewels or something. Fluttering above all of this was their soccer flag, on a broomstick Fred had 'borrowed' from the kitchen.

"Great!" Wilma looked rather jealously at the boys' masterpiece. "We should build something like that sometime."

"Nah…nothing but work!" Melanie sighed as she let herself drop on her back. "Right now I don't want to do anything. No walk on the beach, no museum, no graveyard, no digging up of ghost-coins, nothing!" She squinted into the sun. "Just look at that sky. Endless." She sighed again as she folded her hands behind her head. "Could someone pass me the chips?"

"This picnic was a great idea," Trudie said. "Feels great to just sit here." She looked at the sea. "Just imagine living right by the ocean. Must be great, don't you think?"

"I don't know." Charlie took a handful of the soft sand and let it run through her fingers. "I think all that wind and the waves would drive me crazy."

"How?" Melanie giggled. "You're already quite crazy."

"Yeah?" Charlie chucked a fistful of sand on her friend's belly.

"Yuck!" Melanie jumped to her feet and performed a wild

beach dance, trying to shake the sand from her clothes. The *Pygmies* applauded enthusiastically.

"Trudie?" Freya asked. "Would you mind if I invite Matilda over? I mean, it's your picnic…"

"Sure," Trudie said. "Bring her over."

Freya immediately jumped up and trudged over the sand to where Matilda was sitting alone, watching some other kids from their class play ball. She hesitantly followed Freya back to the picnic.

"Now all we need is Nora joining us as well," Charlie mumbled.

"I'd be very quiet, if I were you," Melanie said. "You were the one who drove the poor girl from our room. I heard she's feeling very lonely over there with the bitches."

"Hmph," Charlie grumbled.

Freya gently nudged Matilda to sit down between Trudie and herself.

"Hello!" Charlie said. She tried to look very friendly.

"Hi," Matilda mumbled. She looked around. Melanie held out a chips bag to her. "Chips?" Matilda reached gratefully into the bag.

"Hey, we nearly forgot Trudie's present!" Wilma called out.

Trudie looked her, baffled.

"Is it her birthday?" Matilda asked.

"No, but…" Charlie shrugged, "…we thought she could do with a little celebration."

"Why?" Matilda gave Trudie a concerned look.

Trudie cleared her throat. "My parents are getting divorced. This is my consolation picnic, organized by my best friends. Damn…" she rubbed her eyes, "…I always have to start crying."

"There!" Wilma put a little package in her lap. "Now you unpack this."

"Thanks, but…" Trudie gave her glasses to Melanie, "…could you clean these first for me?"

Melanie got to work immediately, but it wasn't easy with her sandy skirt.

"My parents are also divorced," Matilda said. "They have been for quite a while now."

"Really?" Trudie turned to her with a smile of relief. Her friends' pity was really quite nice, but it was always just her to whom horrible things happened. *'Poor Trudie.'* It felt great to meet someone who was going through the same.

Matilda shrugged. "At least there's no fighting at home, but—you know." She dug her naked toes into the sand.

"Here, Trudie, your glasses," Melanie said.

"Thanks," Trudie mumbled. She fumbled with the bow Wilma had tied around her present. Finally she tore open the paper. Inside was a little box, covered all over with little seashells.

"Oh!" Trudie gently lifted up the box and looked at it from all sides. "It's beautiful. Thanks. I don't know what…"

"You can put Jornsen's coins in there," Charlie said.

"No!" Trudie shook her head. "Definitely not those. I wish I'd never found those things."

"Trudie found three old coins on the beach," Wilma explained to Matilda, who looked a little puzzled. "Blood money from old Jornsen. Did you hear him last night?"

"That creepy laugh?" Matilda nodded. "Sounded like one of those laughing-bags." The *Wild Chicks* looked at each other.

"Do those still exist?" Melanie asked. "My mum told me about those."

Charlie rubbed her nose.

"Ah, Charlie's thinking!" Melanie observed. "Absolute silence, please."

"Where are Trudie's coins now?" Charlie asked. "Did you bring them, Freya?"

Freya shook her head. "They're still on the table upstairs, right where we looked at them last night."

Without another word, Charlie jumped up and dashed off. Wilma followed her.

CHAPTER 17

asping for air, the two of them arrived at their room.

"My alarm!" Charlie panted. "There, the alarm paper is torn."

Two tiny shreds of paper were still stuck to the door and the frame.

"Maybe it's still in there!" Wilma breathed. Instinctively, she took two steps back.

"What's *it*?" Charlie pushed the door open.

No coins on the table. No matter how hard they looked, on the floor, under the chairs, the coins were gone. But there was water all over the floor.

"As if someone in huge wellies walked through here," Wilma whispered.

"Wet prints," Charlie muttered. "Didn't that little man in the museum say something about that? That the ghost leaves wet footprints?"

Wilma looked at her wide-eyed.

"Exactly!" she said. "You think it's…?" She frantically looked around.

"Duh!" Charlie said impatiently. "There's no ghost here. And there *was* no ghost here, either. Because ghosts don't exist. That's something Melanie and I can finally agree on. Nope, I think someone is playing a huge prank on us. Question is—who?" Charlie looked at Wilma. "Did you see whether any of the *Pygmies* disappeared from the beach today?"

Wilma shook her head. "Don't think so. They've been digging like crazy all afternoon. All the time. And then they sat around their soccer flag."

"Hmm." Charlie rubbed her nose. "So they have an alibi. And it couldn't have been them, anyway. They're much too busy looking for clues. Hmm." Charlie nearly chewed through her lip, that's how hard she was thinking. "There's someone else behind this."

"And what if there is a ghost?" Wilma looked anxiously at the wet footprints.

"If there is a ghost," Charlie said, "Then I am a *Pygmy*." She pulled Wilma out of the room and closed the door. "Ghosts go through walls. This one here," she leaned down and pulled off the torn piece of paper, "Came through the door. Like a living human."

"But the wet prints," Wilma said. "Look! They just stop over there, right by the wall, not the door." She lowered her voice. "As if it flew away."

"You're right." Charlie stood up and looked down the empty corridor.

At that moment, Mr. Dustman's door opened.

"The others are still at the beach?" he asked. "It's time for us to go."

They were supposed to go on another walk that afternoon, to some earthworks that had once been dug as a defense against the Vikings. It was probably going to be as interesting as the burial mounds.

Charlie sighed. "Yes, the others are still down there."

"Mr. Dustman!" Wilma leaned in closer. "Trudie's coins are gone. And the floor is full of wet prints."

"Impossible!" Mr. Dustman looked amazed. "Maybe it was the old beach master after all? I wonder what will happen during our night walk."

"Night walk?" Wilma gasped.

"Oh yes, the night walk. Who knows," Mr. Dustman walked with the girls to the stairs, "Maybe we'll finally have a face-to-face meeting with old Lap Jornsen—or whatever is left of him."

"What's left of him?" Wilma was hectically twirling her hair. "You mean, he's no longer...no longer whole?"

Mr. Dustman arched his eyebrows. "No idea. I'm no expert on ghosts. What about it?" He looked at Charlie. "Are you going to tell the competition about this newest incident?"

"The *Pygmies*? No, why?"

"Ah, well," Mr. Dustman looked around. "I better try to find Mrs. Rose. See you later."

"Yes," Charlie mumbled.

She rubbed her nose once more. Quite thoroughly.

"Do we really have to go on that night walk? Tonight of all nights?" Wilma asked. "I'm getting a little scared. Aren't you?"

Charlie shook her head.

"You don't think the ghost is going to come tonight?" Wilma asked.

"No, I don't think so," Charlie replied. "At least, not a real one. But something will happen."

That didn't do much to relax Wilma.

CHAPTER 18

The anti-Viking ramparts really weren't that interesting. Mr. Dustman did try to tell some impressive stories about the Vikings and other pirates, but they were still all glad to get back to their hostel. After dinner, once Fred and Willie had completed their kitchen duties, the *Pygmies* went to play table tennis. The *Wild Chicks* decided to join them. Table tennis was the only sport Trudie liked, and they still had a lot of time to kill until the night walk. Time during which Trudie might have fallen back into her gloomy thoughts. And so they played table tennis rounds for two hours, until their t-shirts were soaked and half their pocket money had been swallowed by the drinks machine. It was great.

Only Wilma sat by herself on the window ledge. She couldn't play table tennis. She got them one drink after another from the machine and kept asking for the time. Melanie made a solemn pledge to teach her table tennis first thing after they got back home.

To Wilma's great relief, the table tennis room was locked at nine o'clock, just as the *Pygmies* had gained a lead of nine to ten, thanks to Steve's prowess with the paddle. Mrs. Rose sent them all back to their rooms with the instruction to be back in the entrance hall by eleven—warm clothes and functioning flashlights obligatory.

"Eleven? Why eleven?" Wilma asked with a slightly shaky voice. "That means we'll still be out there at midnight."

"Are you afraid of the ghost?" Willie staggered toward Wilma, his arms raised. "I aaaam the beeeaaaach maaahaaaasterrrr!"

"Stop that!" Charlie shoved him back angrily.

"I'm not at all afraid!" Wilma shouted.

But she was. Everybody could see it. She was as white as a sheet, as if she were a ghost herself.

"Whatever…let's go!" Melanie pulled Wilma with her up the stairs.

"But I am *not* afraid!" Wilma screeched. "Really, I'm not!"

"Everybody's a little scared of night walks," Charlie said, pushing Wilma into their room.

"Exactly." Melanie switched on the light. "That's the idea of a night walk. It's supposed to be a little creepy."

Wilma looked at her uneasily.

"I was once on a night walk," Trudie told them. "At summer camp. Awful. I nearly peed my pants."

She sat on her bed and reached under her pillow to get the seashell box the others had given her. She carefully placed a satchel of sugar from the teashop, her ticket from the museum, and a pebble from the beach inside.

"At least there's no bushes on the beach," Melanie

said. She yawned as she took off her jumper and started rummaging through her bag. "What am I going to wear?"

"Something bright!" Charlie said. "So we can all see each other."

Nora entered the room together with two other girls. Over lunch, the three of them had discovered their shared passion for solitaire.

"Hi, Melanie," one of them warbled. "Do you already know what you're going to wear for the final night's dance?"

"Sure," Melanie answered. "But I'm definitely not telling you!"

The other girl just shrugged.

"Jeez," Charlie groaned, "Is that all you can think about?"

"You can talk!" Nora said. "I heard you and the *Pygmies* are hunting a ghost with wet feet."

The two girls from the bitches' room laughed so hard, they barely managed to climb into Nora's bed.

"No!" Charlie growled. "We're hunting the one who's *pretending* to be the ghost."

"Oh dear, sounds complicated." Nora joined the other two and started shuffling her cards.

"Charlie," Trudie whispered. "What if there really is a ghost?"

"There are no ghosts!" Melanie said impatiently. "You can bet your life on it, just like old Jornsen." She pulled a black knitted dress over her head.

"I said bright!" Charlie protested.

"I feel like black," Melanie replied tartly. She began to brush her hair. "And it's the warmest I have."

"Could you please listen to me?" Trudie begged. "If there is no ghost, then maybe—maybe," she bit her lip, "That's even more dangerous. Maybe it's a real criminal."

"Oh no!" Wilma pressed her hand over her moth.

"Yep, a criminal who steals a bunch of old coins," Charlie taunted her. "No, there's definitely something else behind this."

"Maybe those coins were incredibly valuable!" Wilma said. "Like rare stamps or something."

"Well, he's got them all back now," Freya observed drily. "And the ghosting will have an end. Now you can all stop driving yourselves crazy. It's really great by the sea at night. Very peaceful, and you can hear your footsteps in the sand and the rush of the waves." She sighed. "Wonderful. I could do this every night."

"Oh dear, she's a romantic!" Nora sighed from her bed.

Wilma and Trudie just gave Freya baffled looks.

CHAPTER 19

B y the time they stepped outside, the wind had picked up quite a bit. The night was pitch dark. The moon only managed to peek through the dark clouds for seconds at a time.

Giggling and shouting, the whole class followed Mr. Dustman and Mrs. Rose down to the beach. There was definitely no chance of hearing your footsteps in the sand, or even the rush of the waves.

"Hey, girls!" Fred called. When Charlie turned around, she looked straight into the beam of his flashlight. The *Pygmies* were trudging through the darkness barely a meter behind them. "In this weather, you really don't have to be afraid of any ghosts. The wind would shred their flappy bodies to pieces."

The *Pygmies* nearly choked on their own laughter. Only Steve kept looking around anxiously. Their flashlights were useless in this darkness.

"Today," Baz intoned with a low voice, "Is the anniversary of Lap Jornsen's death. It's time for him to find a new victim!"

"Stop it," Trudie shouted over her shoulder. "That's not funny."

"Leave it, Baz!" Willie said. "Chickens are afraid of ghosts."

"Yes, they might stop laying eggs!" Steve screeched.

Charlie spun around. "So that's how you keep your word?"

"What word?" Trudie asked.

"Nothing," Charlie muttered.

"Okay, okay." Fred pushed the others behind him. "Just a few jokes. We thought you'd enjoy our company."

"We thought without us you'd be afraid of the dark," Baz added with a broad grin.

Freya shot him an angry glance that immediately switched off his grin.

"Just so that we're clear," Melanie said. "If I have to march through the darkness and the sand, then I'd at least like to get some peace, so I can look at the stars, or listen to the ocean, and feel a little romantic. Okay? With your constant baby squeaks I can't do any of that."

"Oh Melanie!" Fred dropped to his knees and squeezed his hands to where he thought his heart might be. "We are romantic. Truly!"

"Yes, we love the stars and all that," Steve added. "Honest!"

Melanie shook her head, but she did have to giggle a little…very much to Charlie's disappointment.

"Come on," she ordered. "Forget about those idiots."

"We get it!" Fred made a deep bow. "Charlie's not the romantic type. We better take our leave."

"But don't think you can call us back when the ghost comes," Willie said. With that. the four boys sprinted past the single file of marching children and disappeared into the darkness.

Melanie was still giggling. "They are kind of cute, don't you think?" she said.

"What?" Charlie growled.

"Come on," Freya gave her a gentle nudge. "They were just having a bit of a laugh."

Finally there was quiet. Most of the kids walked in silence, or whispered quietly. They pointed their lights at their feet, or at the sea, where the pale fingers of light were swallowed up by the dark waves. The *Wild Chicks* also walked in silence. Charlie had linked arms with Freya, Melanie with Trudie and Wilma. The night sky was huge, and the wind blew away more and more of the clouds, until the darkness above them was only freckled with stars. At some point, Mr. Dustman stopped them. He came walking down the line with a big plastic bag. "I am collecting all flashlights," he said.

"Why?" Trudie immediately hid hers behind her back.

"So that you can for once enjoy the night without artificial light," Dustman answered. "At least that's the reason I'm giving you. I told the boys it was a test of courage. You pick the version you like best. And whoever absolutely does not want to part with their light," he looked at Trudie, "Can of course keep it."

Trudie bit her lip. She looked at Melanie, and then at Charlie—and then she also threw her flashlight into the bag. She just clutched Melanie's arm a little tighter.

"Have fun!" said Mr. Dustman. "We're walking to that dune over there. You should be able to make it out, even without your flashlights. From there, we'll be following the wooden walkway which should lead us straight back to the hostel. Okay? I'll be bringing up the rear of this procession."

With that he walked on to the back.

Charlie turned around. Behind them were only Nora and the two other card girls.

"Where is Matilda?" Charlie asked Freya.

"She's up front, with Mrs. Rose." Freya lowered her voice. "You know what? She and Trudie were talking all through dinner about divorce and parents and all that. I think it's really good for Trudie to see that Matilda has the same stuff to deal with. The only others with divorced parents are boys."

Charlie just said: "Hmm."

Many in their class had parents who were divorced or separated. But Charlie was the only one who didn't even know her father. A weird feeling. *But what good would it do to think about it?*

"Charlie!" Wilma suddenly whispered beside her. "What?"

"Did you hear that?"

"What?" Charlie and Freya stopped to listen.

Wilma was not the only one who'd heard something. The whole class had stopped and was pricking their ears.

"That's just the wind!" said Melanie.

"What kind of wind makes a noise like that?" Trudie whimpered.

They all heard a howl, then a hollow moan. It came across the beach, growing louder and louder.

"The ghost!" They heard Steve scream. "Help! Mrs. Rose! There—the ghost!"

Charlie saw a few dark figures dash off. That was probably Fred, and Willie. One of them still had a light. *Cheats!*

"It's coming from ahead!" Melanie called out. "From that dune."

Charlie ran. She nearly stumbled over her own feet in the dark. But she just had to find out who was trying to play a prank on them all. And if Fred dared to run toward it, then she had to as well. The wet sand sucked at her shoes, making running very hard work. She noticed that others were following her—the *Wild Chicks*.

"Here!" Wilma shouted. "Charlie, I still have my flashlight!"

Relieved, Charlie grabbed it and pointed the beam of light toward the dune. The howling and moaning was getting louder and louder. Ahead there was nothing to be seen, except for the running *Pygmies*. Hold on—Dustman was also running toward the creepy sounds. He was making better progress than the girls. Soon he'd have caught up with the boys.

"Wow, did anyone know he could run that fast?" Melanie panted.

Gasping for air, they struggled up the dune. They stopped on the crest. The *Pygmies* were standing just a few meters away. The ghostly sounds were coming from somewhere further down, from the darkness between the dunes. Charlie and Fred pointed their flashlights down, but their light fell on nothing but sand and sedge.

And still the howling grew louder.

"It sounds horrible!" Trudie groaned.

Wilma looked at the others. "I don't really want to go down there," she said.

The *Pygmies* also seemed to be hesitating.

But Dustman hadn't stopped. Clumsily, his wide coat flapping behind him, he was making his way down the sandy slope.

"What's he doing now?" Trudie was aghast.

"That ghost is going to jump him and pull him under!" Wilma whispered. "Like quicksand. I saw something like that once on TV."

They all stared breathlessly toward the bottom of the dune.

"It's gone!" Melanie suddenly whispered. "Listen! It's gone!"

The four others listened.

They could only hear the wind. The wind and the sea.

They heard Mrs. Rose call: "What's going on up there?" She had stayed with the rest of the class. Only four other children had joined the *Wild Chicks* and the *Pygmies* on their chase.

"All clear!" Mr. Dustman called from below. "Nothing here, except for a few empty cigarette packs."

Without thinking, Charlie tucked the flashlight into her pocket and slid down the dune, to where Mr. Dustman was standing. The others followed, *Chicks* and *Pygmies*.

At the bottom, they all looked around, mystified.

"Nothing!" Fred said, angrily kicking the sand. "There's absolutely nothing here. It's not right." He looked at Charlie. "Did you see someone run away?"

Charlie shook her head.

"But we should have seen someone!" Baz sounded scared. Charlie had never seen him like that.

"Strange indeed!" Mr. Dustman said. "Even if we go with Melanie's theory that this is some kind of tourist gimmick, then we should have at least gotten close enough to whoever is doing this." He looked around, frowning. "After all, we all heard those howls quite clearly, didn't we?"

"We did!" Willie nodded. His face had darkened. "I got goosebumps. I thought Jornsen is going to grab me any moment with his moldy hands."

The others stayed quiet.

"Maybe he just disappeared into the dune," Wilma said with a trembling voice. "Ghosts can probably do that."

"Nah!" Charlie shook her head determinedly. "I bet you, someone's sitting out there in the dark, laughing his head off about us."

"You think?" Trudie moved closer to Charlie and took her hand.

"Charlie might be right, for a change," Fred said. "We're getting punk'd. Big time."

Melanie sighed. "Well, at least nobody can say this was a boring trip!"

"Exactly!" Steve snickered nervously. "The full program."

"Come," Mr. Dustman started back up the dune. "We should get back to the others. Or would you like to poke around in the dark a little more?"

Freya shook her head. "No. What for? If it was a ghost, then we'll never find it. And if it was a person then he won't be hanging around for us to find him."

"Good point!" Mr. Dustman agreed. "For tonight, we'll just have to live with the fact that we couldn't solve the mystery of the hostel ghost. Are you coming?"

That night Charlie didn't sleep a wink. She kept trying to find the connection between the different incidents—the spooky laughter in the night, the stolen coins, and the wet prints that ended by the wall. And now the howls in the dunes.

Outside, a sliver of light was painting the sea red. Suddenly, Charlie had a thought. A crazy thought…

She of course had no way of knowing that Fred was having the exact same thought, at exactly the same time.

CHAPTER 20

The next morning, the weather was perfect. For the last day of their visit, the island spoiled them with sunshine and, for the first time, the sea was actually blue. Even Charlie felt the urge to wade through the waves. The island was trying to make it hard for them to say goodbye.

Trudie looked particularly sad as she looked out of the window.

"It's so beautiful here," she mumbled. "I can't bear to think that we'll be leaving tomorrow."

"So, don't think about it!" Melanie put on her sunglasses and clipped two plastic Minnie-Mouses on her earlobes. "Simple!"

Trudie didn't find that simple at all.

"Is your dress in the Guinness Book?" Charlie asked. "As the shortest dress anywhere, ever?"

"Haha!" Melanie adjusted her earrings. "Not everyone likes running around in the same pair of trousers every day."

"Come off it!" Freya pushed the two of them toward the door. "Let's not start on that again. We're late for breakfast anyway."

The only free table was the one next to the *Pygmies*.

The boys all had dark faces. It looked as if they'd gotten sandworms for breakfast. They didn't even lift their heads when the girls sat down.

"What's gotten into them?" Freya asked.

"Morning!" Mrs. Rose got up and clapped her hands. "Could I have some quiet, please?" She was wearing pink lipstick, as she always did when the weather was nice. "Since we're now all here," she said with a frown at the *Wild Chicks*, "I'd like to announce today's program."

"Program!" Melanie rolled her eyes. "Not another hike!"

Mrs. Rose continued. "We had planned to visit the seal shelter today. But I just learned that it is closed today due to illness. We sadly won't manage to cover all the aspects of the environmental situation here on this trip. But," she gave Mr. Dustman a smile, "We can always catch up on that in class."

"Haha! We probably know more about pollution that him!" Fred muttered angrily. "Why do we constantly have to listen to that stuff? I never dunked a sea bird in oil. I collect every piece of paper and every bit of glass, and what do my parents do? They just chuck it all in the rubbish anyway. Chuck, gone, sorted."

"And off to the ocean with the other shiploads of rubbish!" Baz joined in.

Mr. Dustman grinned. "Oh, I can see you're perfectly informed. I'm already looking forward to reading your essays."

The faces of the *Pygmies* darkened a little more.

"And now back to the program for the day!" Mrs. Rose started again. "I'll keep it short. We thought we might all benefit from a day without a program. This last day is yours. There's only one rule: stay here at the beach. No big excursions without telling us first. And—" she lifted her hand, "Mr. Dustman and I would like to invite you to a beach barbeque this afternoon at three. And tonight, as you probably already know, we'll have our farewell disco from eight to ten."

"Fantastic! No program!" Melanie clapped her hands. "I will actually get to use my new bikini! How about it, *Chicks*? Shall we make the boys wet?"

"Them? Wet?" Charlie said. "They already look like drowned rats."

The *Pygmies* were flopped on their chairs. Steve was performing some trick, but that did nothing to lift the mood.

"What's up with them?" Wilma shook her head.

Melanie squinted with some sudden thought. "Hold on. What day is it today?"

Freya looked at her in surprise. "Saturday. Why?"

"Of course. Oh dear, the poor boys!" Melanie gave the boys a sardonic grin.

"Well, I don't get it," Charlie said. "Are you talking in riddles?"

"Goes to show, you really don't know boys at all!" Melanie leaned over the table and lowered her voice. "Saturday afternoon is live soccer on the radio. I sometimes listen to it. It's quite exciting. I bet the boys never missed a Saturday. And just today Arsenal is playing Man U. Get it?"

"Nope," Charlie replied.

Melanie rolled her eyes. "Arsenal is the *Pygmies'* favorite club, and Man U," she shrugged, "I really can't explain that. Anyway, today is that game, and what were we not allowed to bring to the island?"

"Radios," Trudie said.

"Oh dear indeed!" Charlie shook her head and grinned. "And that's why they're looking like that?"

Melanie nodded. "I bet you anything. Wait, I'll prove it. Hey, Fred!" She turned to the *Pygmies*. "What are you doing this afternoon? Like, between half three and half five? Will you be playing soccer?"

Willie looked at her as though he'd like to tear off her head.

"Don't even start making fun of this, okay? We'll find one!" Fred grumbled. "This radio ban is completely stupid anyway."

"You see?" Melanie winked at Charlie.

"Dustman has a radio," Wilma said. "Maybe he'll lend it to you?"

"Already asked him," Baz mumbled. "That's a no-go."

"Said he hates soccer," Steve squeaked. "And that he was not going to be part of us mushing up our brains, or something like that."

"Mush up our brains," Fred said. "What a joker. I bet the thing's just standing around in his room—when he's not listening to the news, that is."

"But there's a TV in the common room," Trudie suggested. "And there's always soccer playing on Saturday nights. I know that because my father…" she stopped and bit her lip, "… because my father always watches it."

"Well, boys. Bad luck." Melanie got up and straightened her dress. "I'm sure you'll survive."

"Exactly," Charlie added. "And Man U is probably going to win anyway."

CHAPTER 21

The *Pygmies* were barely seen all day. For a while they built some additions to their sand castle, but then they disappeared into the hostel again. Mrs. Rose was lying on her towel, reading a crime novel, while Mr. Dustman stalked through the cold water, with his trousers rolled up, smoking one after another of his stinky cigarettes, only intervening when someone was about to be dunked in the sea fully clothed.

Their last afternoon on the island really was a peaceful one. Melanie spent most of the time lying flat in the sun, unless she had to touch up the polish on her toenails. Trudie, Matilda, and Freya collected seashells and pebbles. Wilma read *Tom Sawyer*, which made her chew down her fingernails with excitement. And Charlie buried her toes in the sand. Her socks were the only clothing she had shed on the beach. She was thinking about the ghost again.

Finally, after she had buried and excavated her feet exactly thirteen times, she finally said: "I think I know who it is."

"Who is what?" Melanie mumbled without opening her eyes.

"The ghost." Charlie squinted into the sun.

"Let me guess," Melanie said. "It's…hmm…yes, it's

Mr. Applecurd, the little round man from the museum. He gets so bored in his museum that he's started to play ghost in his free time."

"That's not it!" Charlie threw a handful of sand on Melanie's green toenails.

"Hey!" Melanie gasped. "Those weren't dry yet. Now I have to start all over. Or do you think I want sandpaper toenails?"

"Anything is better than that moldy green," Charlie replied.

Melanie stuck her tongue out at her. "You don't know what you're talking about. But go on, who's the ghost?"

"Nope." Charlie shook her head. "I have no evidence. Just deductions, you know?"

"Suit yourself," Melanie sighed. "Maybe you get some evidence tonight. I'm sure the ghost will make a farewell appearance."

"Definitely." Charlie looked at the hostel. "Wonder what the boys are doing. They better not be putting any beach worms into our beds."

"No way!" Melanie rubbed her toenails. "They've got other problems. I bet they're running around, asking anyone who might lend them a radio."

"I'll go and check anyway." Charlie got up and shook the sand from her trousers.

There were few things as boring to Charlie as hanging around on a beach. Weeding in her gran's garden, for example.

And she already had to do that quite often.

Charlie ran through the hostel's entrance hall. She looked at the large clock. Half past two already. The *Pygmies* didn't have much time left. As she jumped up the stairs she heard Steve's voice. Nobody but him made that screeching sound. Charlie ducked as she snuck up the last steps. She peered around the corner. There they were. All of them together, and they definitely looked guilty. Charlie could spot that a mile off. But the *Pygmies* were not standing by the *Wild Chicks'* door. They were at Dustman's door. Willie and Fred had their backs turned to her and were keeping an eye on the corridor, while Steve and Baz were kneeling in front of the door, fiddling with something.

"Come on, Steve!" Fred said from the corner of his mouth.

"We should leave it be," said Willie. He was uneasily shifting his weight from one foot to the other. "Seriously, Fred. This is attempted burglary. It won't pass as one of Steve's little magic tricks. If my father hears of this he'll beat me 'til I'm blue and black."

"I told you to stay in the room," Fred hissed. "Did I or did I not?"

"Got it!" Steve squeaked.

Dustman's door opened. Baz scurried inside, and quickly came out again with Dustman's radio.

Charlie held her breath. *Had they gone completely mad?*

"Wow, this is a real boombox!" Willie whispered. "It's got a

CD player and all." He took a step back and raised his hands. "Man, take that back inside. If anything happens to it, we'll all be kicked off the school."

"Who's going to find us in the broom cupboard?" Fred hissed. "Nobody knows us down on the first floor. And we don't have to sit in front of the radio all the time. One of us stays on the beach and keeps an eye on Dustman. We swap every fifteen minutes. Quarter past five, right after the final whistle, Steve takes it back to Dustman's room. Agreed?"

"Agreed," Steve said.

Baz wedged the huge radio under his arm. The *Pygmies* all walked toward the stairs.

That's when Charlie finally got up.

"You know what?" she said. "You've really lost it now."

The *Pygmies* turned even whiter than the wall.

"Jeez, Charlie!" Fred panted.

"She's going to rat us out!" Steve squeaked. "And we'll all get booted off the school."

Baz was nervously licking his lips. And Willie looked as if he was ready to drop dead any moment.

"I'm not a rat!" Charlie said huffily. "But you should bring that thing back right away. Where are you taking it anyway?"

"To the broom cupboard on the first floor," Steve mumbled meekly.

"We're just borrowing it," said Fred. "For the game. We'll take it right back afterwards."

"You're mad!" Charlie spun around on her heels. "Completely gaga. But I never saw you."

"And? Any beach worms in our beds?" Melanie asked after Charlie returned to the beach. She had put on her dress again. "A bit too cold for a bikini," she said. "Those there, playing in that icy water, they must have Eskimo blood or something."

"The boys stole Dustman's radio," Charlie said.

Melanie looked at her, dumbfounded. "Not possible."

"Yes!" Charlie let herself drop into the sand next to Melanie. "Just for that silly game. And now they're all sitting in some broom cupboard. Crazy, hmm?"

"Where is Dustman?" Melanie asked. "Haven't seen him in a while."

"I did," Charlie muttered. "He's put on some goofy apron and is over by the picnic spot, barbequing sausages, while Mrs. Rose is dishing out potato salad on paper plates."

"What? And Big Steve is sitting in some broom cupboard instead of helping himself to some sausages? They really are keen on that game!"

"I won't let those idiots ruin my appetite," Charlie said. "Dustman's sausages smell quite nice. How about we get ourselves a portion? Freya, Trudie and Wilma are also on their way. Or are your toenails still not dry?"

For that Melanie chased Charlie all the way to the barbeque.

Trudie forewent her sausages. And her potato salad. Instead, she nibbled on some crisp bread. Steve appeared soon enough and helped himself to a huge portion. He kept a close eye on Dustman, while munching one sausage after another. But the teacher was fully occupied with keeping a steady stream of sausages coming off the barbeque. After fifteen minutes Baz appeared, looking rather glum, and took Steve's place.

"And what are they going to do if Dustman does go upstairs?" Wilma mumbled through a full mouth. Charlie had of course told them all about the *Pygmies'* radio heist.

"Are they going to trip him over or what?"

Trudie nearly choked on her crisp bread.

After Baz, it was Willie's turn, and then came Fred. The boss of course took the last shift, as usual.

Meanwhile, Mr. Dustman had sat down at a table with Mrs. Rose. He was drinking a beer and eating a sausage, recuperating from the strains of barbequing. Every now and then, he lifted his weird apron to wipe his lips with it.

Suddenly Wilma gave Charlie a nudge. "He's out of cigarettes," she whispered. "See?"

Dustman fished his box of cigarettes from his shirt pocket. He looked inside and then threw it on the table.

"Oh no!" The *Wild Chicks* looked at Steve, but he was distracted by his third helping of sausages.

Dustman stood up and squeezed past Mrs. Rose's knees.

"Holy…they'll get kicked off the school if they get caught!" Freya breathed.

Steve was still busy with his sausages.

Charlie quickly jumped up. "Mr. Dustman!" she called.

Dustman turned around.

Steve gave a start and dropped his half-eaten sausage.

"I just wanted to ask you something," Charlie looked Dustman straight in the face. "Do you think the ghost will come back tonight?"

Mr. Dustman looked at Charlie for a moment. Then the left corner of his mouth curled up into a smile. "I am certain of it!" he said. "Considering how successful it was yesterday."

Charlie was still looking at him. "I hope it'll do a bit more than yesterday."

Dustman shrugged. "Who knows! Maybe howling and moaning and scratching at doors are all it can do. I am no ghost expert, just a poor little teacher."

He turned around again.

"Mr. Dustman!" Trudie called. "Those cigarettes, really, they are very unhealthy."

Dustman turned around once more.

"You're right there," he said. "But they are my only vice, and everybody should be allowed one, don't you agree? But," he looked at the blue sky, "Maybe I really should just enjoy the clean seaside air and give my lungs a break."

"Exactly!" Charlie said. "Very smart."

Mr. Dustman gave her a wink and sat down next to Mrs. Rose again.

"Phew, that was close," Wilma groaned.

"You can say that again," Melanie rolled her eyes. "Those dunces definitely owe us now."

At that moment, Baz appeared. He whispered excitedly in Steve's ear, then walked toward the *Wild Chicks'* table.

"And?" Melanie nudged Freya. "Is this another love letter delivery?"

Freya blushed, but Baz leaned down to Charlie.

"Fred says you should come up."

"Does he?" Charlie gave him a wary look. "Trying to boss me around as well now, is he?"

Baz made an exasperated face. "Could you just come up, please?"

"Where? To the broom cupboard?" Charlie shot a quick look at Dustman, but he was obviously busy with getting the second round of sausages on the barbeque.

"Yes, we found something interesting, and Fred thinks you should listen to it."

"Ah!" Charlie didn't get it.

"Are you coming, or not?" Baz drummed his finger on the table.

Charlie got up with a sigh. "Yes, yes. But if I'm not back down here in ten minutes, the others will come and get me.

Understood?"

Baz just nodded tersely. He quickly ran ahead, back into the hostel, up one flight of stairs, and down the strange corridor, until they were standing in front of a narrow door. Charlie could hear faint voices behind it. Baz knocked twice, and then once more. Then they quickly slipped into the darkness.

The *Pygmies* were crammed like sardines around Dustman's huge radio.

"What's the score?" Baz asked.

"Don't ask!" Willie answered. "It's a total disaster."

"And what am I doing here?" Charlie asked.

"Listen to something," Fred said. "As a little thank you for not ratting us out."

"Quite a big thank you, if you ask me," Willie growled. "But of course nobody ever does."

Fred switched from radio to cassette. Then he pressed play.

Lap Jornsen's ghost howled and moaned out of Mr. Dustman's radio.

Charlie grinned. "I knew it!" she said smugly.

"What?" Fred looked crestfallen. "You're not surprised?"

Charlie shook her head. "I kind of made some deductions, but I had no proof."

"Well, we do," Willie grumbled. "Dustman is the ghost, and the *Pygmies* won the bet."

"You can't prove anything," Charlie corrected him. "Or

should we go to Dustman and say: 'hi, we just borrowed your stereo and guess what we found'?"

"She's right," Fred said. "But at least we now know who's been playing tricks on us. That's something, isn't it?"

"Right," Charlie nodded. "And thanks for sharing. But now I'd like to get out of here."

"And I want to hear the end of the game!" Baz muttered.

"Okay, okay!" Fred switched back to radio—a deafening scream of "GOOOAAAAAAL!" flooded the little cupboard.

"By whom?" Steve nearly swallowed his tongue with excitement. "By whom?"

Charlie quickly made her exit.

CHAPTER 22

"**D**ustman!" Melanie was leaning over Trudie, snipping away at her fringe. "I still can't believe it."

Freya stood in front of them, holding Melanie's travel mirror. Trudie was staring into it, watching rather worriedly as her hair got shorter and shorter.

"Okay, now a little gel," Melanie said, "And you'll look totally cool."

Trudie did not seem convinced.

And none of them had any gel. Melanie never used any on her locks.

"But I have lipstick," she said. "And eyeliner, and even a little bit of mascara. See?"

"I'm not sure," Trudie mumbled. "I think…I'd rather stay the way I am."

Wilma stormed into the room, totally out of breath.

"Dustman's hidden the stereo. Between the rubbish bins, right where we'll all walk past when we walk back from the dance tonight. You'd never know if you didn't know where to look. But I know exactly where it is." She plopped herself into a chair. "So what do we do now?"

"I've thought of something." Charlie was sitting on her

bed, dangling her feet. "But we need the boys."

The others looked at her with surprise.

Charlie explained her plan.

Shortly after, Wilma did a messenger run to the *Pygmies*. Willie was going to play a particularly important part in Charlie's plan. One might even say he'd be playing the leading role.

The disco took place in a separate building, which stood at a distance from the main house and was therefore perfect for noisy events. Inside there was a small dancefloor, surrounded by chairs and tables. There were posters (quite old ones) on the wall, and a stereo with a cassette player and a turntable, but no CD player, as Steve observed scornfully. The lighting consisted of some spotlights for the DJ and red lightbulbs around the room. Next to the stereo was a pile of cassettes, for everyone in the class had brought their favorite music to the party. The teachers had brought the drinks, and there was food in the form of huge bags of chips, though most of them were still quite stuffed from Dustman's afternoon sausage fest.

The *Wild Chicks* were last to arrive at the party. After completing the preparations for Charlie's plans, Melanie had scrounged some hair gel from the bitches' room to spike up Trudie's new haircut. The result wasn't bad at all. After that, Melanie had to change her outfit three times, until Freya and Charlie grabbed her suitcase and locked it into the wardrobe.

The other three *Chicks* went dressed exactly as they had been all day, their chicken feathers around their necks, and their trousers still shedding sand from the beach.

Charlie did notice, however, that Freya smelled somewhat more flowery than usual. Melanie always smelled smashing anyway.

The *Pygmies* were already there as the girls filed into the dark room. The four of them were in a great mood, for the goal that had fallen in the broom cupboard had been scored by their team. Even Willie was looking less grim than usual, though that might have had less to do with the soccer game than with the fact that Charlie had given him such an important part in her plan. Steve was wearing the bowtie and the suit he always wore when he performed on children's birthdays. Fred had hung a tiny dried crab from his ear, instead of the little earring that was the Pygmies' gang sign. It made him look quite the pirate.

"Where's Baz?" Freya asked.

"Somewhere behind that pile of cassettes," Willie replied. "He's volunteering as DJ."

"Oh." Freya fidgeted with her chicken feather. "Then I'll go and say hello to him." She shot a quick, sheepish glance at Charlie before pushing her way through the crowd toward the DJ platform.

"He wrote her at least four notes," Melanie whispered.

"Four?" Charlie shook her head. "I only saw one."

"Yes!" Melanie arched her eyebrows. "You never notice these things."

"Hey Trudie," Steve said. "We, erm, have something for you." He took off his weird magician's hat, reached inside, and produced a long seashell necklace. "Abra Kadabra! It's a real charm against sadness. Works nearly one hundred per cent of the time."

"Oh, thanks!" Trudie breathed. She carefully put her head—and her new haircut—through the necklace. She grinned broadly, "I really don't know what to say."

"Never mind," said Fred. "Willie made it." He pointed to his earlobe. "Just like my earring."

"Great!" Melanie said. "I'd love one of those."

"No problem!" Willie mumbled. He was looking awkwardly at his hands.

"And what about our bet?" Steve asked, making his bowtie spin like a propeller.

Charlie shrugged. "I'd say it's a tie. We're kind of on the same team now, aren't we?"

"Then how about this," Fred suggested. "We carry your luggage to the train, and we also get to dance, each with our favorite chicken."

"Perfect!" Melanie batted her eyelids so hard that Charlie could hardly bear to look at her. She felt herself blush all the way up to her hairline. But luckily nobody could see that in the dim light.

Trudie chewed her lip. "That probably means you all want to dance with Melanie."

"Not necessarily." Steve giggled a little too hysterically. He let his bowtie spin some more.

"Won't work anyway," Charlie said harshly. "We're five, and you are four. That means one of us will be left over. That's not fair."

"Well, I wouldn't mind dancing with two *Chicks*," Steve squeaked. He was quite hyper this evening.

Charlie looked at the others.

"I'm okay with it," Melanie said.

"Me too," said Wilma.

Trudie just nodded.

"Fine." Charlie sighed. "Whatever. It's quite obvious who Baz is going to pick." She looked around. Freya hadn't come back yet, though Baz was already getting busy at the turntables.

The bright lights went off. The room was flooded in a red glow, and the music started up so loud that Mrs. Rose nearly fell off her chair.

Steve took Wilma by his left hand, and Trudie by his right, and led them to the dancefloor.

Willie looked at Melanie, looked away again, and then looked at her again. He couldn't get a word out.

Melanie giggled and tossed back her locks. "Well, do you want to dance or not?" she asked.

Willie muttered something indecipherable. Then the two of them disappeared off toward the dance floor as well. Only Fred and Charlie were left standing between the empty tables.

"Sorry about that," Charlie grumbled. "Seems like I'm all that's left."

"And?" Fred asked. "I wanted to dance with you anyway."

"What?" Charlie asked.

Baz cranked up the volume even more.

"I wanted to dance with you anyway," Fred screamed. "But I can't really dance."

"Me neither!" Charlie screamed back.

And both had to laugh. And then they tried to dance together, anyway.

The party was supposed to last from eight to ten—and then the room would have to be locked up again. At five minutes to ten, the electricity went out. Suddenly, it was dark and quiet.

"Don't panic!" They heard Dustman's voice. "We probably just blew a fuse. Let's all quietly and calmly go outside."

Whispering, everybody felt their way through the narrow doorway. Neither Fred nor Charlie could make out any of their gang members in the dark.

"This is probably the cue for Dustman's final ghost show," Fred whispered in Charlie's ear. "I bet you he fiddled with the electricity, to make it all the more spooky."

"Yes. Just as well we prepared everything before," Charlie whispered back. She held on to Fred's sleeve, so they wouldn't be split up as well. "Good old Dustman is going to have the surprise of his life. I wonder how he's going to switch on that big radio."

"No idea," Fred replied. "At first I thought he has a remote. But I think he just turned the thing on at the beach, before we left for our walk. The whole tape is full of moaning and howling, so it didn't really matter when we walked past it."

"I think we better all go back to the hostel," Mrs. Rose called. "We can only clean up tomorrow anyway. I'll tell the caretaker about the electricity."

"I'll do that!" Mr. Dustman said eagerly. He quickly stalked off in the direction of the hostel. Nobody paid any attention to where he went, except for the *Wild Chicks* and the *Pygmies*.

Halfway to the hostel, Mr. Dustman suddenly disappeared between the rubbish bins.

"Ah, he's turning it on now," Fred whispered.

Steve pushed toward them with Wilma and Trudie. Willie, Melanie, Baz, and Freya had also appeared out of the crowd.

"Looks like we're all here," Baz said. "Let's roll."

Mr. Dustman was already walking toward them again, his face all innocent. The class pushed past him, laughing and shouting. They were just a few meters away from the rubbish bins.

"There!" someone called out. "I hear something. The ghost!"

The same howling and moaning that they had heard the previous night at the beach. Everybody froze and listened.

Suddenly, however, the groaning stopped and a deep voice howled: "Duuuuustmaaan! Duuuustmaaan, where are you?"

Everybody turned to look at Mr. Dustman, who was making quite a stupefied face.

Freya had to press her hand to her mouth to keep herself from laughing out loud.

"Dustman!" the creepy voice continued. "You have disturbed the peace of my grave. You stirred the spirits of my victims, and now they are haunting me!"

"Wow, Willie," Melanie whispered. "That sounds great!"

"You sound like a real dead man!" Wilma agreed. "Like a real corpse."

Trudie nodded. "I've got goosebumps all over."

The others obviously felt the same. Nobody had moved. Nobody ran toward the voice, to check where it was coming from. Not even Mrs. Rose.

"Dustmaaaan! I am warning youuuu!" the voice continued. "You will not let these innocent children write any essays about me, or I will visit you every night and throttle you with my bony hands."

"Okay, okay, I give up!" Dustman called out. He raised his hands, while Willie's voice continued to threaten him with sleepless nights, bony fingers, and ghostly revenge.

"I admit it all!" Mr. Dustman announced. "I was the ghost. Okay?"

"You?" Mrs. Rose looked dumbfounded. "It was you? Scratching at the doors, that filthy laugh, the howling at the beach?"

Dustman nodded. "I plead guilty! The coins and the bits of fabric were mine. I had planted some more things, but sadly nobody found them."

Mrs. Rose started to laugh. She laughed so hard that she gave herself a hiccup.

Willie's voice was still moaning in the background. Charlie ran between the rubbish bins and switched off Mr. Dustman's radio. Mrs. Rose was still giggling when she returned.

"You of all people, Mr. Dustman!" she said. "You of all people!"

"Yes." Mr. Dustman looked a bit hurt. "And?"

"It's mean!" Mrs. Rose bit her lips. They were coral red. "It's mean that you didn't let me help you."

Now Mr. Dustman was completely confused.

"I would have had first-class haunting ideas," Mrs. Rose continued. "Definitely. I am deeply hurt. How are you going to make up for this?"

Abashed, Mr. Dustman pushed his hand through his sparse hair. "I don't know. Maybe on the next school trip?"

"A bit feeble, but okay." Mrs. Rose nodded. "I will make

sure to remind you."

"Mr. Dustman!" Fred said. "Does Lap Jornsen actually haunt this island? Or was that all made up?"

"No, no, he really is supposed to haunt these parts," Mr. Dustman tucked his earlobe, "But I just moved him from the other side of the island to here." He shrugged. "Call it creative license."

"On the other side?" Wilma looked at Mr. Dustman with round eyes. "He's actually haunting on the other side?"

The *Pygmies* groaned.

"Forget about it, Wilma," Charlie said.

"Sorry, but I have to ask." Mr. Dustman looked around. "Who blew my cover? Was it the *Wild Chicks* or the *Pygmies*?"

Charlie and Fred looked at each other.

"Both," Fred said. "Together."

"Indeed? Is that so? Interesting." Mr. Dustman smiled his most self-satisfied teacher smile. "Then that just leaves one question. Whose creepy voice did we just hear? I do assume it wasn't old Jornsen's."

"That was Willie," Melanie said. "He sounded quite spooky, didn't he?"

"He did!" Mrs. Rose gave Willie a surprised look. "You seem to have hidden some real talent from us."

"Nah!" Willie grumbled. He looked as if he'd love to dive into the sand and disappear.

"No, really. Quite remarkable," Mr. Dustman chimed in.

"Much more talented than me. We should recruit you for the drama club."

Willie squirmed with embarrassment.

"And who wrote his script?" Mrs. Rose asked.

"Charlie," Wilma said. "She wrote it all down, we got the key to the party-hut…"

"…which was much easier than we had expected," Fred interrupted her. "We just said we needed to get things ready for the party tonight."

"And then," Wilma continued, "We just recorded over Mr. Dustman's tape."

"They're not half as dumb as they look," someone said from behind.

Charlie turned around. That was Nora. When she noticed Charlie looking at her, she quickly pulled a face.

"Great!" Mrs. Rose clapped her hands. "I say we now all put our ears to our mattresses. Agreed? After all, we all have to get back on that horrid ship tomorrow."

"Oh no!" Trudie moaned. "Did she have to remind us? Now she ruined the whole evening."

"No way!" Melanie put her arm around her shoulder. "We'll distract you. You'll see."

CHAPTER 23

The *Wild Chicks* didn't go to sleep. While Nora snored happily on her bed, the five girls sat on Charlie's bed, ate chips and chocolate, and looked at the ocean.

They had opened the window wide so that they could get a farewell whiff of the salty wind. As it got cooler inside, they just moved closer together.

"If time could stop right now," Trudie said quietly. "For, like, a week or so."

Freya nodded. "You know what I sometimes wish: that you could put a time like this into a jam jar. And when you're sad, you can just open the lid and get a noseful of happiness."

"Yes," Charlie agreed. "We should have a whole shelf full of them. A jar of school trip, a Christmas jar, one with sunshine, one with snow…"

"And a big jar of *Wild Chicks*," Wilma added.

They sat some more in silence, looking at the waves. The rhythmic rush of the water soon made them sleepy.

Melanie was the first to yawn. She put her head on Trudie's shoulder.

"Oh no," Trudie sighed. "I just remembered that we have to go on that awful ferry tomorrow."

"Always keep your eye on the horizon," Melanie mumbled.

"Always helps."

"And how did you keep your eye on the horizon while you were below deck at the games machines?" Charlie asked sleepily.

"Got me!" Melanie giggled. "But I heard it works a treat."

"Who told you?" Wilma asked.

Melanie brushed a stray lock from her face and yawned. "Fred and Willie."

"Oh dear!" Wilma rolled her eyes. "Great sources of wisdom, those two."

"Freya?" Melanie asked. "Baz and you, are you a couple now?"

Freya didn't answer. She lay, rolled up like a kitten between the others, and was fast asleep.

"Well, we'll probably have to get Wilma to spy on them for us," Charlie said. "Or we'll never find out."

Wilma folded her arms and frowned. "I'd never do something like that. Definitely!"

"Never mind," Charlie nudged her. "I was kidding."

"Jeez!" Melanie listened toward Nora's bed. "Listening to her snoring. If she ever gets married she'll have to buy her husband earphones."

"And? You talk in your sleep," Charlie replied.

"I don't!" Melanie twiddled with her locks. "You're just trying to yank my chain."

"No, it's true!" Now it was Trudie's turn to snicker. "I heard it, too."

Melanie blushed.

Charlie put an arm around her shoulder. "I just couldn't make out what you were saying," she whispered in her ear. "Big bummer."

"She did giggle in her sleep, though," Trudie said.

"And you know what you do?" Melanie asked. "You pull your duvet up to your nose so that your feet poke out at the bottom. And Charlie rolls around so much in her sleep that she ends up completely uncovered, with just her stuffed chicken on her face."

They all nearly fell of the bed with laughter. And Freya slept peacefully through it all.

"And I," Wilma looked eagerly at the others. "What do I do?"

"You?" Charlie got to her knees, pushed her face into the pillows and stuck her bum in the air. "You do this."

"Stop it! Stop!" Melanie gasped. "That's exactly what she does."

That's when Freya finally woke up. She rubbed her eyes and mumbled, "What are you laughing about? Not about me, I hope."

"No," Charlie replied. "You sleep normal. Like a little kitten."

"That's good." Freya closed her eyes again and rolled herself up even more. "Tell me when we're there," she mumbled. "This stupid ship is really quite rocky."

That was it.

Wilma laughed so hard that Melanie only just managed to prevent her from falling off the bed.

"That's one we forgot," Trudie said when they had all managed to calm down a little. "A jar full of laughter!"

"Yes, but then we can't have any Baz jokes in there," Charlie said.

"The boys are put in a jar of their own," Melanie suggested. "For special occasions."

"Stop it!" Trudie rubbed her mouth. "All that laughing is making my lips ache."

"I once read about a man who laughed himself to death," Wilma said.

"What a great way to die!" Charlie took her chicken and rolled up really close to Freya. She closed her eyes. "This really was a great trip," she mumbled. "I just hope Dustman is not going to ruin it and make us write an essay about it all."

"He probably will," Melanie yawned. "Could someone close the window?"

But the others were already fast asleep, Freya and Charlie with their heads at one end, Wilma and Trudie at the other.

Melanie yawned again as she climbed out of the bed and tiptoed to the window. She took one more look at the sea and then crawled back in with the others. She found herself a tiny free spot, with Trudie's toes under her nose and Charlie's elbow in her back. But she was soon also fast asleep.